Refracted Reflections

Twisted Tales
of
Duality & Deception

Compiled and edited by
Kaye Lynne Booth

WordCrafter Press

Introduction by Kaye Lynne Booth

Compiled and edited by Kaye Lynne Booth

Cover by *WordCrafter Press*

Introduction

When I was a kid and the carnival came to town, my favorite thing was the funhouse, because it always had a house of mirrors, the funny kind that bend and distort my image, reflecting and refracting my image to look like something different and unusual. It was fun to try and find the true me in those images, which often looked silly and made me laugh, but some were so distorted that they looked like something not altogether human, and those mirrors created images which were even a little scary.

Mirrors reflect true images, or so we're taught to believe. But certain mirrors reflect something else; something altogether different, and we can't always rely on our own senses to find the truth within. Some images reflected back at us are deceptions. With some, like the reflections from the funhouse mirrors, it's easy to tell that what we're seeing isn't real. But in others, it's more difficult to tell what is truth, or reality, and what is illusion.

Sometimes, when we look in the mirror, we see a different side of ourselves, one we don't recognize. If there are two sides to every coin, there are multiple sides to every person and multiple points of view to every interaction, every relationship. The stories within these pages tell of those types of reflections; the refracted kind that reveal the inner dualities and deceptions.

The Mirror Guardian

Elisabeth Caldwell

There was something under Kella's bed. A mean, nasty, horrifying something.

The dark shine of blood dripping from her ankles was proof of it.

An odd laugh escaped her lips as relief mixed with terror. If the thing under her bed was real, then she wasn't delusional. No matter what that pompous ass of a shrink had to say. But, if she wasn't delusional, and the thing under the bed was real, then he was real.

He. Was. Real.

Too bad she had to be attacked by an under-the-bed-dwelling monster to figure it out.

Kella wracked her brain to remember anything Calon had told her that could explain the creature under her bed. She came up blank. She'd have to ask him what the hell was happening.

While crouched in the middle of her bed, she scanned the room for her handbag. The moon provided plenty of light since she didn't have curtains. It was hard to find window coverings that worked with curved windows, and curved windows were what you got when you lived in a tower. Fairytales never focused on details like that.

Kella spotted her purse on her nightstand. She leaned over and snatched it, careful not to let any of her limbs hang over the edge of the bed. She sifted through the contents as quietly as she could.

Where the hell was that little makeup mirror?

She normally hated looking in the mirror. Hated the image of her shiny, too white scalp, and features that were too large and wide to be considered pretty.

The thing under the bed snarled.

She dumped the bag, no longer caring about the noise. Wallet, keys, pens, lip gloss, scrunchie, mints, band-aids, but no mirror.

Crap. Crap. Crap.

The mirror must have fallen out of her purse when she'd dropped it earlier. That explained the creature under her bed. It had to be a Daemon. Calon had told her that Daemons could travel through mirrors... but she'd thought that wasn't real.

Because she'd convinced herself Calon wasn't real.

Because that's what the doctor had told her.

He'd also told her it wasn't surprising a 33-year-old, big boned, unmarried woman with alopecia would create an alternate, imaginary life where she was fated to bond with a magical warrior to protect the world. Or at least her little piece of it. He'd said it was her way of making herself feel important.

He'd also said it wasn't surprising her fantasy lover was tall, dark and handsome, since it was unlikely she'd ever attract a man like that in real life. Kella hadn't told him that tall meant seven feet. That dark meant ash gray skin, thick as leather, and just as soft. That handsome meant impossibly high cheekbones, fingers and toes that curved into pointed claws and glorious periwinkle wings that shimmered in flight and felt like a cocoon when they wrapped around her.

The growls grew louder, and the bed shook.

She'd have to make a run for it.

Kella caught a glimpse of her reflection in one of the windows as she prepared to leap off the bed. The curve of the window softened the image, but her white scalp was still shiny and stark.

Being bald sucked.

She jumped off the bed and raced to the rectangular bathroom inside the circle of her bedroom. She was fast, but not fast enough. The Daemon slashed the back of her right upper thigh. Pain made her vision swim, but she continued to run, slamming the heavy, oak bathroom door behind her and dropping the 2'x4' style barricade into position. She'd thought the ancient style door lock was another of her aunt's eccentricities, but now she knew it was there to keep Daemons out.

The mirror over the vanity shimmered. Calon was coming. He always knew when she needed him. His sharp-boned, craggy face appeared first, followed by his angular, muscled torso. Long grey fingers with black claw-like nails extended through the mirror. She was supposed to reach out and take his hand. That's what she'd done every other time he'd come to her over the past few months.

But this time she was nervous. This time, she couldn't pretend he was a dream.

Kella rubbed a large, tanned, short-nailed hand over her cool scalp, wishing for a scarf or a baseball cap, but those were all back in her bedroom.

Calon waved his hand, beckoning.

This was no time for vanity or girlish nerves. She was bleeding all over the bathroom floor, and there was a Daemon scratching at the door.

Kella squared her broad, muscled shoulders and reached into the mirror.

When their fingers touched, she was instantly transported into Calon's study. He lived in a tower like her own. The room was warm and inviting despite the stone walls. Bright flames flickered inside the glass doors of a wood burning stove. Thick, colorful, woven rugs covered the floor. A heavily cushioned couch faced the stove, and there were books everywhere. Everywhere. On shelves. On tables. Even piled on the floor.

This was her favorite place.

"I made a mistake. I lost track of a mirror, and now I have a Daemon in my tower."

She felt foolish, bursting out the confession like a schoolgirl who'd come home with a demerit.

"Any mistake you live to learn from is a good one," he answered in his warm, rich, smooth-as-milk-chocolate voice. "You're injured."

"They're just scratches."

Scratches that felt like her legs had been torn off.

Calon pushed her gently toward the couch. She'd been the tallest girl in every class since the fourth grade. It was odd to have to crane her neck so far to look up at him.

"Lay down."

She followed his instruction because her legs hurt like hell, and she knew he could heal her. His smooth claws were gentle on her skin as he inspected her ankles, then moved up higher, pulling her torn pajama pants apart to examine her wounds. Her breath hitched as one claw gently grazed her inner thigh.

"This is awkward."

Calon leaned closer, his breath tickling the sensitive skin so close to her bottom.

"Awkward and embarrassing."

"What's awkward?" Calon asked. "Why are you embarrassed?"

Why was she embarrassed? Maybe because half her butt was hanging out?

"I'm not small," Kella said.

"Why would you want to be small?"

She arched her head off the couch. *Could he really be this dumb?*

"Small girls don't have cellulite."

"Mirror Guardians are never small. If you were small, you wouldn't be as strong or fast as you are. You would be useless against the Daemons."

He was always so matter of fact. Once. Just once, she'd like to see him ruffled.

He held out a low, round jar containing a thick brown paste. "You do it."

Kella rose from the couch, annoyed.

"What's in it?"

"You tell me."

He was always testing her. She snatched the jar from his hand, unscrewed the cap and sniffed.

"Chamomile, calendula, yarrow, and...," Kella inhaled deeply, "plantain."

Calon's face exploded in a wide smile, exposing pointed teeth. Her annoyance disappeared, and her heart fluttered.

Literally fluttered.

I am so ridiculous.

Kella lowered her gaze and focused on rubbing the medicine on her leg while chanting the healing spell Calon had taught her. She let out a deep sigh as the skin knit back together and the pain receded.

Calon nodded approvingly and handed her a wet towel. She cleaned the blood from her ankles, thigh and hands then set the towel in the wash basin.

"So, now you believe?" he asked.

Kella nodded affirmatively.

"Then you're ready."

"I am *not* ready."

"You are," Calon insisted.

She wasn't ready. She was never going to be ready. Because being ready meant she'd never see Calon again.

"There has to be another way."

Grief flashed in Calon's eyes, and his expression grew sober. "This is the way it has always been. The Keeper trains the Mirror Guardian. When the Mirror Guardian is ready to stand on her own, she returns to her tower and destroys all the mirrors. You must never allow a mirror into the tower again."

"I'm not breaking all my mirrors. I'm not giving you up. I can't. I won't."

Calon's lips flattened in disapproval. "We've talked about this. The only way for Daemons to enter your realm is through mirrors in the towers. Into a mirror in a tower in this realm and out of a mirror in a tower in yours. We Keepers fight to prevent the Daemons from entering our towers, but sometimes they get by. You saw that today. I have no idea how that Daemon got through to you. It could have burrowed into the basement, broken a window, snuck in while I was out gathering wood. I'm vigilant, but I can't be everywhere all the time. If you destroy the mirrors in your tower, the Daemons will never get through."

"So, I'm just supposed to walk away and never see you again? Never know what happens to you? What if the Daemons come and you can't fight them off?"

"Then the Masters will send another Keeper to guard this tower."

It was too much. Too much to think that she'd never see Calon again. That he would remain in his tower fighting Daemons to protect her world.

That he might give up his life doing it.

Kella paced, finally stopping in front of the old-fashioned oval, free standing mirror Calon always pulled her through. The ancient wood glistened. The mirror was so old, her reflection was slightly warped, but she looked tall and strong.

"Who came up with this shit system anyway?"

Calon's frown deepened. "I've never heard of any Mirror Guardian as difficult as you are."

"What about my aunt?" Kella asked.

She'd barely known her aunt. Kellianne was actually her great aunt. Her grandmother's crazy, hermit-like sister, who'd lived in a tower on 400 acres in the Allegheny mountains with no phone or internet. A tower Kella had grown up hearing about but had only seen in pictures. Her family had been puzzled when Kella inherited the tower when her aunt passed and enraged when she refused to let them come visit.

The tower was precious. A beautiful structure on beautiful grounds. She'd felt the magic the second her feet crossed the property line. Her family wanted to gawk at it like carnival goers at an old-time freakshow.

Never going to happen.

Calon took her tanned, calloused hand in his own larger, bonier, gray one. His grip was strong and leathery, yet gentle.

"I never met your aunt. The prior Keeper knew her. When a Keeper shares his magic with a Mirror Guardian, he becomes linked to her, bonded, connected. A Keeper can only share his magic once. Once he does, the Keeper's life is connected to that Mirror Guardian. He only lives while she does."

The words Calon hadn't spoken hung in the air like wet fog. The prior Keeper had died when her aunt had died.

If she died, Calon would die.

Kella shuddered and closed her eyes. Maybe the doctor was right. Maybe she was delusional.

But would a delusion combine the roller coaster stomach roll of learning someone else's life depended on your safety with the sweet euphoria and warm heat of that same someone's hand in your own?

Calon lifted her fingers, pressing his lips firmly against her skin, and her eyes fluttered open.

Kella reached up and grabbed two of the hooks atop his wings, pulling them toward her.

"This is a bad idea," he whispered, but didn't fight her.

He always said it was a bad idea. Every kiss. Every embrace. Every late-night flight while she clung to his muscled back, the edges of his wide, shimmering wings brushing against her legs, the wind cool on her face.

Kella watched in the ancient mirror as his thundercloud-purple wings enveloped her. There was nothing like the satin heat of those wings encasing her body. She felt safe. Wanted. Loved.

A howl and the sharp crack of wood shattered the moment. Calon shoved her away. She tried to grab hold of something. Anything. Her fingers closed on air.

Whomp!

Her back struck the cold tile of her own bathroom floor, knocking the wind out of her.

"Watch out!" Calon's voice traveled through the mirror.

She leapt up and flipped into the claw foot tub, landing on her feet like a cat.

Thud.

A large wooden chest flew through the mirror, falling so hard it cracked the floor.

"Break the mirror!" Calon yelled.

The sounds of snarling growls and breaking furniture echoed off the walls of the bathroom.

"Break the mirror! Now!"

The howls grew louder.

"Now, Kella. Now!"

With a cry of anguish, Kella smashed her fists into the mirror. Over and over and over. Then she sunk to the floor in despair.

For hours, she could not move. The pain in her heart eclipsed everything, until, finally, she noticed the blood. Blood dripped from hundreds of long cuts on her hands and arms. She should be dead. A person could not lose so much blood and survive. But she wasn't an ordinary person. Calon's magic ran through her veins.

Kella rose slowly. A distorted, fractured face looked back at her. The mirror was splintered and broken. Hundreds of shards littered the sink and the floor. One large chunk created a bridge between the vanity and the tub.

She'd been lucky.

Daemons were only awake during the night, and it had been near dawn when Calon shoved her back through the mirror. He must have held them off until the sun rose. If he hadn't, she would have been killed. A Daemon could not travel through a cracked mirror, but each broken piece that had fallen was now its own individual mirror. Countless Daemons could have entered her tower.

She needed to get moving. Clean up the mess. Calon had explained so many times what was expected and why. Trained her for this moment. For what she would have to do when the time came, and she'd done it.

She'd broken the mirror. Done the right thing. Done her duty.

So, why did she feel like a miserable piece of over-chewed gum stuck to the bottom of a sneaker?

Because she had abandoned Calon.

Calon, who had taught her how to fight. Calon, who had taught her how to grow herbs and make potions. Calon, who wrapped her in velvet soft wings in front of the wood burning stove telling her stories she'd thought were myths. Calon, who made her feel loved and accepted. Calon, who was willing to give his life for her own.

Her lungs hurt thinking about it.

Needing a distraction, Kella opened the chest, leaving streaks of blood on the worn wood.

She knew what it contained. She and Calon had packed and unpacked it together during the months of nights she thought he was a dream. It held the tools of a Mirror Guardian. Lightweight armor. Weapons. Seeds to grow herbs. Books of recipes and incantations. Jars of homemade potions. These were the tools she was supposed to use to protect her realm.

The rules were clear. Train daily. Practice. Stay alert. Cultivate herbs. Make potions. Be ready to fight. Keep everyone else away. And, most importantly, keep no mirrors. Safeguards upon safeguards. If she followed the rules, the Daemons would never enter her realm, and all would be well.

Calon had told her stories that had been passed down to him about Mirror Guardians who'd become lax. Who'd allowed guests in their towers, and those guests brought mirrors. Guardians who'd allowed repairmen into their towers, and those repairmen brought mirrors. Guardians who'd given up and left their posts, and others had moved in and brought mirrors.

Those were supposed to be cautionary tales. Cautionary tales for a cautionary life.

Kella did not want to live a cautionary life.

She tugged out a small jar of mixed herbs. The same mix of herbs Calon had given her last night. She rubbed the gritty, aromatic paste on her arms and hands. The cuts healed quickly with a sweet, relieving heat. She rinsed the blood from her skin in the sink.

She picked up a large, ivory handled, surgically sharp knife from the chest, then slid the heavy bar lock on the door to the side. A sleeping Daemon lay just outside the door. She approached cautiously. It felt wrong to kill a living being, especially in its sleep, but she had no choice. If the Daemon escaped, it would use its incredible sense of smell to track down the nearest humans and feed on them. She couldn't let that happen.

Up close, the Daemon was immense, cat-like with grey-green scales that acted as armour. Each of its four limbs had six razor sharp claws, and jagged teeth filled its mouth. She crouched and swiftly ran her knife across the soft fur at the Daemon's neck. It was one of the creature's few vulnerable spots. The blade sliced through trachea, esophagus, carotid arteries and jugular veins. Calon had taught her this was the quickest and most painless way to kill.

She took a moment to wish the Daemon's soul a journey of peace, then hurried to the bed to retrieve the makeup mirror. Mirror in hand, she returned to the bathroom and lifted a large wooden mortar and pestle out of the chest. She put the makeup mirror in the mortar, then added all the small mirror shards from the sink and floor, grinding all the pieces into a fine dust, ensuring no Daemon could ever pass through them.

Next, Kella gingerly lifted the large chunk of the broken mirror, careful not to cut her hands on the rough edges. The rules required she smash it and grind it up, just as she'd done with the small pieces. Instead, she propped it on top of the vanity and stepped back to study her reflection. Her jaw was square. Her eyes were fierce. Her curved stomach and thick thighs didn't appear fat. They looked strong.

"A strong enough will can always make a way."

Her aunt's words shimmered in her mind. She'd only seen the woman a few times, but every time Kella had seen her, she'd repeated those words.

Kella did not want to live a cautionary life.

She was strong. She was fast. She was smart. She'd been trained by Calon, so she'd been trained by the best.

She turned back to the chest, rifling through the contents, gathering the items she needed.

She replaced her torn pajamas with thick, shiny, silver leggings and turtleneck. Calon told her the material was handwoven by witches. It would never tear and was impervious to Daemon teeth and claws. He'd laughed when she'd called it mithril.

Kella slid a hood of the same material over her head, and topped it with a lightweight, metal band that circled her head. For once, she was happy she had no hair. If she did, the hood would feel hot and sit oddly on her head. She layered on a dark green belted tunic and slipped leather boots on her feet.

She turned toward the mirror.

A Valkyrie stared back at her.

"A strong enough will can always make a way."

Kella would not choose rules over loyalty.

She would not allow the man she loved to sacrifice himself for her.

She slid her quiver on her back, grasped her bow in one hand and her sword in the other. She inhaled a deep, calming breath and dove through the mirror.

On the other side, she found Calon in his own armor preparing for battle.

"You came back," he said with steel in his voice, but joy in his eyes.

"How could I not?" Kella answered. "I am a Mirror Guardian. I am a protector. I will not abandon my Keeper. I will not abandon my heart. We will rise and fall together."

Calon slid strong, leathery fingers down her cheek, then brushed his lips lightly against hers.

"We will rise and fall together."

Elisabeth Caldwell

Elisabeth Caldwell grew up a Philly (and suburban Philly) girl with thick glasses and her nose buried in a book. When she was 12, she fell into the yellowed pages of one of her grandmother's Mary Stewart novels and has been obsessed with reading and writing ever since. She sees fairies in the trees, mermaids in the ocean, ghosts peeking out the windows of sprawling Victorians in Cape May, and a story behind every couple that walks by holding hands. She writes poetry, short stories and novels.

Elisabeth lives in Bucks County, PA with her three vibrant children, a husband who is her soulmate and best friend, and one very sweet, albino corn snake. She practices law by day, writes by night and daydreams every chance she can get.

The Cost of Magic

Keith Hoskins

Kenzia of Ravenstone stood outside the small, unremarkable hut. Weary from travel and feeling the autumn chill starting to bite, she wrapped her cloak more tightly around her and pulled her hood snug over her golden hair. After several ten-days of travel, Kenzia's trek had finally brought her to the home of the person she sought: Grand Sorceress Masilda; the one person who could grant her greatest desire.

Kenzia approached the meager structure tentatively, not convinced this hovel was the home of a mighty sorceress. She took a deep breath and knocked. Moments later, a small window-like door, set inside the larger one, opened to reveal the head of a small humanoid creature.

"What do you want?" asked the creature in a cantankerous tone. Despite its size, the creature's voice was deep and gruff. His face filled the tiny portal, and his long nose protruded through the opening like an accusing finger. His floppy ears drooped forward onto his bald head, and his bulbous eyes scrutinized Kenzia as he looked her up and down. Kenzia recognized the small, grumpy being as a dour gnome.

"My name is Kenzia," she told the dour gnome. "I come all the way from Ravenstone to request an audience with Grand Sorceress Masilda. I'm in need of—"

"No Masilda here," the creature snapped. "Now bugger off." His head pulled back, and he began to shut his little door.

"Wait," cried Kenzia. "I have money." She unfastened a purse from her belt and shook the bag, letting the unmistakable sound of gold clanking against gold grab the crotchety gnome's attention. "I can pay for her services... if she is able to help me, that is."

The creature pushed his face through the opening, letting his nose drift toward Kenzia's purse. He gave it a few sniffs, and his eyes widened.

"Let her in, Bonker," came a woman's voice from inside the hut. "No need to let the poor girl stand out there all day. Where are your manners?"

Bonker gave a brief sneer, stepped back, and closed his tiny door. Then Kenzia heard the sound of metal on wood as multiple bolts and latches were released from their catches.

The door creaked open. Kenzia refastened her coin purse and stepped through the threshold. Once inside, Bonker closed the door behind her.

The interior of the hut was five times—maybe ten—that of what the outside of the dwelling had led Kenzia to believe. Each of the four walls were at least thirty feet long, and the ceiling vaulted to more than half that. Though large, the dwelling was anything but spacious. The far wall hosted shelves filled with bottles and canisters that, no doubt, contained the sorceress's reagents needed for her magic. The other walls were covered by objects of various sizes and shapes, and undetermined purposes. And what didn't have a home on one of the walls, sat on the crowded floor, while others hung from the ceiling by ropes or chains. Kenzia gawked at the menagerie of objects surrounding her. There were so many other ordinary—as well as extraordinary—things.

Kenzia smiled as she took it all in. *Now* this *is the home of a powerful magic-user*.

"Welcome my dear," said an older woman who sat in a plush, high-backed chair, almost lost in the jungle of objects around her. "I am Masilda, grand sorceress to the god Dhylames. Please, make yourself at home." She gestured to a chair adjacent to hers.

Next to Masilda lay a creature that made Kenzia take pause. It resembled a wolf, but much larger. It had dark gray fur, and a mane that extended from its head to its bushy tail. Pointed ears stood atop its head, and fangs as sharp as spear tips flanked its massive bat-like maw. Though it lay on the floor, Kenzia imagined the beast would stand no less than four feet at the shoulder, and was easily seven feet long.

Its fiery eyes watched the newcomer suspiciously as Masilda gave it a comforting pat on the head.

"That's an interesting dog you have there," said Kenzia as she took the offered chair, trying not to show her nervousness.

"Oh, Vlestapis is not a dog, my dear. He's a barghest. Savage creatures—and quite intelligent." Her hand reached over and scratched the beast's ear. "I raised him from a whelp, ever since his mother died at the hands of a mountain troll. He's been my loyal companion ever since. Haven't you, my pet."

"Yes, mistress," said the barghest in a gravelly voice.

Kenzia's gaze went from the fearsome creature to Masilda herself. The sorceress wore gold-trimmed purple robes—those of a high-tiered grand sorceress. The robes signified that, not only had she studied all her life to attain her stature in the world of magic, but she had also endured countless tests and trials of her skill and expertise.

Masilda's face was milky white with hardly a blemish. Her black brows and rosy cheeks gave color and life to her alabaster-like skin. A single streak of gray cascaded through her onyx-black hair like a perfect river of silver that not only hinted at her age, but also her dignity and grace. She was a striking woman, though Kenzia guessed that she was in her fifties—about twice Kenzia's age.

Bonker approached the two women, carrying a small table which he placed between them. "Shall I put tea on, Mistress?"

"Yes, Bonker," Masilda said, her grating voice showing irritation toward the creature. "You should have done so as soon as our guest had entered." She shooed him away with a few flicks of her hand.

The dour gnome grumbled something under his breath, then turned and exited through a curtained egress in the middle of the wall of reagents.

"You must forgive Bonker's surly manner," said Masilda. "He's never been quite the same since his brother, Dopnop, died."

"Oh, dear. That must have been difficult for him."

"Yes. Poor thing. But I guess it's my fault, really. I needed a few dragon scales for a spell, and I sent Dopnop to fetch me some from Emberside's mountain lair—completely forgetting how much mountain dragons love the taste of gnomes. But I couldn't have gone myself, of course; that dragon hates me more than anything in the world."

Kenzia gave a sheepish smile and took a sip of her tea.

"Now," said the sorceress, "what does a young woman such as yourself need from the all-powerful Masilda?"

"Well," Kenzia began, "I have some... competition, which I need taken care of. I was hoping you would be able to assist me."

The corners of Masilda's mouth raised. "Ah, I see. A rival for a love? Why don't you just plunge a dagger into her back? Quick and simple."

"Oh, no. I could never do that. I'm not that type of person."

"Very well," Masilda said. "I have potions that you could slip into her drink ..."

"No," Kenzia shook her head. "I would never be able to accomplish that. Actually, I was hoping for something a bit more subtle—and death is out of the question—it would draw too much attention. And besides, she has protection."

"Guards?"

"Yes."

"Magic?"

"Possibly."

"This could be tricky, indeed." Masilda's eyes looked away as she pondered the possibilities.

"Am I asking the impossible?"

"Impossible? Ha!" Masilda scoffed. "Nothing is impossible for a grand sorceress. However, the more intricate the spell, the more expensive the cost."

"That's fine," Kenzia said, setting her purse on the table. "I have money. There's enough gold in there for a score of spells. If you can help me, it's all yours."

Masilda eyed the plump bag on the table, her gaze focused with greed. "I see," she said with a razor thin smile. Then her face took on a more sober visage. "The money is all well and good, but that's not the only cost I was referring to. There will also be the cost of the magic."

"Cost of the magic?"

"It's the first rule of magic: A mortal price must be paid for a mystical prize."

"So, what would the cost be to me?"

"That all depends upon the magic that is used. Usually, for simpler spells, the cost comes from the reagents. More powerful spells require some type of sacrifice to be made to appease Dhylames, the god of magic. For very intricate spells, the cost is extracted from the caster in some form of personal penance."

"Now, you wouldn't be casting a spell directly, since you are not a witch yourself. And since potions are out of the question, I would need to give you an item imbued with a spell. With such an item, much of the cost of the spell will most likely have already been paid by the magic-user who enchanted it. I'm sure I have something in my possession that may suit your needs." Masilda looked around, her eyes darting across the cluttered room.

Bonker walked back in, carrying a tray of rattling china cups and containers. He placed the tray on the table and began pouring the tea.

"Honey?" he asked Kenzia.

"Please," she replied. After he placed a dollop into her cup she said, "Thank you, Bonker," and gave the dour gnome a sincere smile.

His gruff expression seemed to soften a bit, as if kindness was a foreign concept to the small being. "Here's some biscuits for you, as well." He pushed a wooden bowl covered by a cloth towards her.

"Very kind of you."

Bonker turned to his master. "Mistress?"

"What ...? You know what I like, Bonker," she snapped. "Don't waste my time with stupid questions."

Bonker put some honey in her tea, gave Kenzia a quick glance, then headed back through the curtained doorway.

"One possibility comes to mind," Masilda said to Kenzia. "Would you be able to touch this woman? Hold her hand for a few seconds?"

"No. I seriously doubt that."

"You're not making it easy. Perhaps you should just hire a ranger and have her shot with an arr—" A devious smile crept on her lips, and her eyes narrowed. "Tell me .... Is this woman beautiful?"

"Yes, she is."

"Is she vain?"

"Most definitely. I would bet my bag of gold on it."

"Excellent," Masilda said. "I have just the thing. "Wait right here." Masilda stood from her chair and walked to a corner, where she began rummaging through chests and crates.

Vlestapis's eyes followed its master as she went off in search for the enchanted item. Then the beast turned its attention to Kenzia. "Perhaps when my mistress is finished her business, you could stay for dinner." The barghest licked it chops, its eyes feasting upon her.

After a few minutes, Masilda cried out in triumph. "I found it!" she proclaimed as she raised a wooden box over her head. She walked back to Kenzia, the wooden box cradled in her arms like a coveted prize. She reclaimed her chair and placed the box on her lap, a self-satisfied grin on her face.

With one hand steadying the miniature wooden chest, the other reached into her robes and produced what appeared to be a key... a key made out of—

"Is that a finger?" Kenzia asked, her face contorted in a disgusted grimace.

"This is Skeleglass. Made from the finger of Guild Master Phrik, head of the most powerful thieves guild in Tangmire City. It can open any lock in the universe."

The tip of the "key" was brass and had the notches and grooves of a standard key, but the rest of the morbid instrument was a magically preserved digit, complete with skin and knuckles. Masilda inserted it into the lock and gave it a turn. Immediately, the brass latches glowed and sparkled, then sprung open. Masilda replaced Skeleglass back into her robe then opened the wooden box.

With grace and reverence, she removed a silver, gem-encrusted rod. One end of the rod was flattened into a broad oval as if made from clay and run over by a large wagon wheel. When the sorceress turned the rod over, exposing the other side of the flat oval head, a brilliant, reflective surface was revealed.

Kenzia leaned closer. "It looks like... a mirror."

"This is no ordinary mirror." Masilda placed the box on the floor then held the silver item in both hands with the respect she deemed it to be due. "This is the Mirror of Transference."

"Mirror of Transference? So, it's magical?"

"Magical? Silly girl, this is one of the most powerful items in my possession. Perhaps one of the most powerful in the land." Masilda turned the mirror over in her hands, her eyes venerating the item in its beauty and power. Then, she caught her image in the flawless reflection and began to admire her own beauty as well. "Magnificent, isn't it?"

"Aside from being a mirror, it doesn't look special—not magical, I guess is what I'm trying to say."

"That's the whole idea, my dear. Most enchanted items appear as they normally would. Common folk such as yourself cannot tell the difference between them and ordinary items. And every enchantment is different; they come in such varied degrees of power and purpose. Some items—such as weapons—can be used over and over again with their magical imbuements still attached. And some, like this mirror, have a single magical purpose. And once that purpose—that task—is complete, the enchantment is no more, or in this case, evolves."

"And what is the purpose of this particular mirror?" Kenzia asked. "What did you call it—the Mirror of Transference?"

The corner of Masilda's mouth raised like that of a trout being hooked by a fisherman. "Whoever looks upon their reflection at the time the mirror's spell is activated, becomes trapped in the mirror realm—a prisoner of one of the multitudes of magical planes of existence."

"Oh, my," Kenzia said, her fascination and interest growing by the second.

"Not only does the person become trapped in this other plane," Masilda continued, "but everything that was theirs is transferred to the person who activates the spell. All that remains after her imprisonment would be yours."

"You mean, I would get all her possessions?"

"Not only her possessions, but everything that made this woman who she was. You would gain her rank in society, her status, her power. Everyone will accept you as this woman. Essentially, you will *become* her, while still retaining everything that was you. So, if the man you love was torn between the two of you, he will then be yours completely."

"Sounds too good to be true. What's the catch? Or the 'cost', as you put it?"

"The cost, at least one part, would be a single drop of blood on the back of the mirror. Simple and neat. Once the drop is placed on the mirror's silver backing, the magic words to activate the spell will appear. The rest of the cost, however, is a bit more severe." The sorceress paused and lifted her eyes from the mirror to meet Kenzia's. "It will take half of the years from the age of the victim and add it to the age of the spell's recipient. It's called the half-life curse."

Kenzia stiffened, and her eyes widened.

"A logical price to pay, if you ask me." Masilda smirked at the irony, then added, "And the transference is not immediate. It could take up to an hour for the spell to complete its task. So, you will need to determine the proper time and place for this to occur."

Kenzia thought about the cost of the magic a moment. Did the benefit she would inherit outweigh the cost? Aging half the years of her rival was a significant price to pay, but would it be worth it to obtain what she desired? The answer was easy.

"I'll take it." Kenzia smiled confidently and held out her hand for the mirror while pushing her purse toward the sorceress with the other.

"Oh, I'm afraid," Masilda said with a saddened voice, "that the piddly amount of gold you have in that bag won't be enough. Not for something as precious as the Mirror of Transference. For me to give you this, you will have to sweeten the deal significantly."

"But there's almost a hundred gold pieces in that purse," Kenzia pleaded. "You could buy a score of mirrors with so much."

"Perhaps, child. But not *this* mirror." Masilda set the magic item on her lap as if to emphasize her stance. "And to achieve what you are hoping to do... this is your only option." She rested a hand on the mirror and stroked the barghest's head.

Kenzia slumped back into the chair, feeling defeated. She hadn't come all this way just to have the answer to her problem inches away, yet denied due to this woman's greed. But what choice did she have? She needed the mirror, and she would do whatever it took to obtain it. Fortunately, she had come prepared for such a complication.

Kenzia reached for a hidden pouch inside her cloak and removed an object clenched in her fist. "If I include *this,* would we have a deal?"

Masilda eyed Kenzia's closed hand. "That all depends on what it is you grip in those scrawny fingers of yours."

Kenzia opened her hand. Nestled in her palm was a finely cut, multi-faceted ruby, the size of a kobold's egg.

"Oh, my," said Masilda, not bothering to hide her surprise and awe at the marvelous jewel. "How magnificent. I'll wager Emberside himself doesn't possess a ruby like that in his hoard. How did you come across such a gem?"

"It's been in my family for generations. It was given to me by my grandmother on her deathbed. She made me swear to never part with it."

"Yet, here you are, so eager to part with it."

"Not so eager," Kenzia corrected. "But desperate, perhaps."

"You must desire this man greatly to travel so far and give up so much."

Kenzia nodded. "I would do anything to get what I want."

Masilda let out a sigh and gave Kenzia a pitiful look. "Foolish, but I was once in your shoes." Then her eyes scanned the items, appraising what was being considered. Her gaze went from the ruby, to the bag of gold, then to the mirror.

"So, do we have a deal?" Kenzia said, her voice tinged with both hope and anticipation.

Several agonizing seconds passed before Masilda responded. "Yes. I believe we do."

The sorceress reached for the ruby, but Kenzia closed her fingers around the gem, pulled her hand back, and raised her brow. Masilda conceded the unspoken condition and handed the mirror to Kenzia, who then, in turn, handed her the ruby.

The sorceress turned the gem over in her hands, admiring its perfection. Her smile and eyes widened as she held the jewel, letting the light from the candelabra overhead dance on its facets. "Rubies are the most magical of all gemstones. The enchantment possibilities for this are endless. I will have to give great consideration to my plans for this little beauty."

"I'm glad you are pleased."

Masilda forced her gaze from the gem to notice Kenzia staring at her. "What's the matter? What are you staring at?"

Kenzia quickly looked away. "Sorry, I shouldn't have been staring. It's just that ...."

"Just what?" the sorceress demanded. "Spit it out, girl."

"Well ... you have a mole on your cheek. I could have sworn that it wasn't there earlier."

"A mole? Where?" Masilda felt at her face with her fingers, then grabbed the mirror from Kenzia and began scanning her skin.

"*Bortikai-malifee-porazum.*" Kenzia pronounced the magical phrase perfectly, and the mirror glowed in Masilda's hands.

Masilda's eyes widened in terror. She flipped the mirror over to see a drop of blood smeared on the silver backing. Above the crimson mark were the magical words Kenzia had just recited. Masilda's fear-stricken gaze went to Kenzia who held up a small dagger with one hand and a fingertip oozing blood on the other.

"You insolent bitch," sneered the sorceress. "How dare you." Masilda tossed the mirror and ruby onto the table and began to cast a spell upon Kenzia. But she soon found her voice uncooperative, and she could barely utter a gasp, let alone words in the language of magic.

A visage of surprise and horror overcame Masilda as the enchantment of the Mirror of Transference commenced and began to claim its victim.

Kenzia watched in amazement as Masilda's body floated into the air and took on a ghostly form, allowing Kenzia to see through the doomed woman. Masilda thrashed about in a futile attempt to hold onto anything around her, but she was no longer a part of the corporeal world and unable to physically touch anything or anyone.

Vlestapis sprang to attention; it watched helplessly as its master seem to struggle with an invisible foe. Its head went side to side, unsure of how to help the sorceress.

"So sorry for the deception, my dear," Kenzia said to the floating phantom form of Masilda. "But you see, you were the competition I sought to eliminate. Like most magic users, I'm a bit ambitious. And I guess I'm a bit impatient as well. But thanks to you providing the means to remove you from this world, I can now take your place as Grand Sorceress."

Suddenly, a brilliant flash emanated from the mirror, as if it reflected the light of a hundred suns. Kenzia shielded her eyes from the glare, but did not completely look away, for she had to see the spell complete its task to the end. The light grew in intensity and engulfed the grand sorceress.

Then, as abruptly as it had appeared, the light was extinguished, leaving the room dark by comparison. Kenzia's eyes tried to adjust to the normal illumination of the room as she looked around for the sorceress, but there was no sign of Masilda anywhere.

"What have you done?" growled Vlestapis. He bared his teeth, and his eyes burned with hatred. "You will pay for that." The beast crouched on its hind legs, ready to pounce on the defenseless Kenzia, its dagger-like fangs ready to sink into her flesh.

Kenzia fell back into the chair and reached into her sleeve to retrieve her hidden wand, hoping she would have enough time to cast a defensive spell. But Vlestapis was too quick, and the sorceress's faithful servant leapt into the air. As the barghest sprang towards its intended victim, another brilliant flash occurred, then the massive creature was gone and replaced with a tiny ball of white fur that landed in Kenzia's lap. It was a pup, and it yipped at Kenzia, confused and afraid.

Confused herself, Kenzia looked up and saw Bonker with a wand of his own raised and pointed to where the barghest had last been. He lowered the wand and gave Kenzia a sheepish grin.

"Wand of Transposition," explained the dour gnome, bowing his head respectfully. "I knew the foul beast would give you some trouble, so I had it change places with that winter-wolf pup you're holdin'. Vlestapis is probably runnin' for his life from that little one's momma."

Kenzia looked down at the tiny canine, then back at Bonker. "How did you know? About my intentions, I mean."

"When I smelled your bag, I could tell the coins inside were only gold-covered copper. I suppose I more hoped than actually knew what you were up to."

Kenzia gave him a wry smile. "Very good, Bonker. Quite clever."

Then, Kenzia felt a heaviness in her chest, and her balance seemed off to a point that she might topple out of her chair. The mirror awakened once again, and light poured out of the looking glass and bathed Kenzia in a warm beam. Her head swam as memories and knowledge, that were not her own, filled her mind at an incredible rate. Spells ... potions ... magic of every kind became known to her as if they were hers to begin with. What had taken Masilda decades to learn, took only seconds for Kenzia to absorb. More and more poured into her, so much so, and at such an accelerated rate, that she wondered how much more she could possibly take.

I will take it all! Kenzia grimaced as she endured the severe influx of knowledge like a tiny brook being fed by a mighty waterfall. She *would* take it all; the spell gave her no choice in the matter.

However, it wasn't only her mind that was being altered; her body was changing as well. Her skin began to lose its taught and smooth texture, her hair began to thin and gray. *The half-age curse,* Kenzia realized. *The mirror's cost.* But she did not fear, for an added twenty-five years or so wasn't so bad. By the time the mirror finished, she should be no older than Masilda had been. *Perhaps even a few years younger.*

But something was wrong. Kenzia felt her body growing older, but it didn't stop at just a few wrinkles. She began feeling pains in her joints, her skin pruned like a rotting piece of fruit. Her hair went from golden locks, to gray, to stark white, then it fell out altogether. She doubled over as her back failed her, then toppled as her knees gave way. Seconds later, she collapsed onto the floor, curled up and writhing in pain as her body continued to deteriorate. Finally, all that remained of the woman from Ravenstone was a pile of dust.

It was over. The mirror's beam ceased, and the artifact lay still on the table.

* * *

Bonker stared at the pile of dust on the floor. It took him a few seconds, but he finally understood what had happened. Masilda had been four hundred years old and had used powerful spells all these years to keep her young and alive. When the mirror's spell demanded payment, it had aged Kenzia two hundred years. The poor woman never had a chance.

But at least Bonker was free. His disparaging master was gone, and he had the place to himself. He reached down and picked up the pup and stroked its head. "We'll be just fine here, you and me. Just fine indeed."

The house began to tremble. Various objects around the room swayed and shook from the quake. Some fell to the floor while others clanged against each other. Bonker steadied himself against a large caldron, not understanding what was happening around him. Then, the mirror rattled on the table surface and came to life once again, bathing the room in light. Bonker closed his eyes and turned away.

When the room finally became still, and the light faded away, Bonker turned back around and was astonished to find someone standing before him.

"Mistress?" said Bonker as he set his incredulous eyes upon Masilda.

The grand sorceress ignored the dumbfounded dour gnome and looked down upon the powdered remains of Kenzia. "Foolish girl," she spat. "To think she could outsmart me; Masilda, Grand Sorceress to Dhylames. I'm like the seasons; powerful, revered, and I always come back."

"But... how...?" Bonker managed to get out.

Masilda flashed him a grin and held up Skeleglass. "I told that girl this key could open any lock. And not just ones with tumblers and springs." She looked back down at the dust on the floor. "Such a feeble attempt by an inferior creature."

Bonker couldn't believe his bad luck. This woman was his curse. He feared he would never get out from under her cruel dominance over him.

"Clean up this mess, Bonker," Masilda demanded. "And bring me some dinner. I'm famished from this annoying ordeal."

"Yes, Mistress," Bonker replied, and then set the wolf pup on the floor.

"Oh, and Bonker..."

"Yes, Mistress?"

"Vlestapis..." She gestured to the white, wide-eyed pup. "Return him. Immediately. I'll decide on a fitting punishment for you, later." Masilda sat in her chair, clearly exhausted as she leaned her forehead onto the fingertips of one hand and cradled the large ruby with the other.

"Yes, Mistress." Bonker produced the Wand of Transposition from his pocket and pointed at the unsuspecting pup. He hesitated then gave his master a hateful glare. Just before he unleashed the spell from the wand, an insidious smile crept upon his face. As a precaution, he took several steps back.

In a flash, the pup disappeared and was immediately replaced by a creature of immense size. But it wasn't the fearsome barghest that took its place. Instead, a gargantuan beast with green scales, leathery wings, and a long snake-like neck filled the entirety of the huge room. The mountain dragon smiled as it looked down at the trembling Masilda.

The grand sorceress gawked at the wyrm—her mouth agape, and her eyes the size of the gemstone she still held in her hand. "Emberside," was all the grand sorceress could say or do as the dragonfear gripped her and had her paralyzed.

"Hello, Masilda," Emberside hissed. His eyes narrowed with purpose, and an ironic grin stretched across his reptilian face. Then his massive head reared back as he took in a considerable breath and prepared to unleash his fiery death upon the hapless sorceress.

"For Dopnop," Bonker said as he fled through the back, barely escaping the all-consuming flames.

Keith J. Hoskins

Keith J. Hoskins is a short story author, award-winning poet, and founding member of the Bel Air Creative Writer's Society. He has four short stories in four anthologies as well as his own anthology, Beyond the Portal. Keith is currently working on his first novel: Kray and the Coveted Seer, a fantasy novel set in a magical world. Keith's main genres of interest are fantasy, science fiction, and thrillers.

Always

By Ligia de Wit

Bali stepped through the grasslands, spear at the ready. Hot soil burned into the soles of her bare feet. She tightened her grip on the spear, alert for any sudden movement that would signal her quarry.

Helios shone in the sky and beads of sweat trickled down her neck, glimmering on her tawny skin, to the strip of sand-colored cloth wrapped around her breasts. Other huntresses adventured around different paths, so this piece of the Isle of Veralius belonged to Bali.

There was a scuffle to her left, and Bali lifted her weapon, expectant. Her nostrils flared. There! The two-meter-long lizard had spotted her, flicking its forked tongue. Sharp, curved claws dug into the earth, its short, sturdy legs belying its swiftness. It lunged at her.

Bali screamed in defiance, holding her ground.

She slid to the side and stabbed before the creature could crash into her. The spear's obsidian tip broke through the scaly green-gray skin right below the neck. The lizard thrashed and lunged at her legs trying to bite her with its sharp teeth.

"Don't," she panted. "Gaia has lent me Her strength, for I am Her Huntress, and you, my offering."

Bali's grass skirt brushed her knees as she squatted next to the struggling lizard. She drew the dagger from her belt and plunged it into the creature's neck.

"May Gaia and Helios provide you with a quick death," she recited. "For you are part of the Cycle, and the Cycle is part of us."

The animal lost strength, blood seeping from its back and neck. She seized its jaws using a rope prepared just for this purpose and tied it off.

More than one careless huntress had lost a leg when they didn't follow the ritual as tradition dictated.

"Let your blood taint the soil"—she retrieved the dagger and cleaned it on the ground—"and my skin."

She dipped her fingers in the lizard's blood and smeared two lines of it on her cheeks then repeated the same on her arms and thighs.

"May Gaia choose me and take me beyond." *Beyond Veralius and into the mythical land of Primanus, Gaia's abode.*

The distant snorts of wild boars wafted in the hot breeze. Whistling a huntress tune, she fetched her sled and placed the fat lizard on it. *What a mighty hunt!*

She knelt by the sled. "Gaia," she recited, her head low and arms loose at her sides, "my people and I thank you, for the Cycle will be benefited with this hunt."

The air shimmered before her and, unsteadily, she rose to her feet. She thought she saw her reflection on it. Was Gaia choosing her? Then Bali realized it was the normal shimmer caused by the heat and not Gaia's Portal. Gaia opened Her portal every other generation for one lucky woman to travel to mystical Primanus, where she would conceive a male child to infuse new blood to the tribe.

The other huntresses were gathered beneath the shadow of two gigantic jacaranda trees, a short distance from their village. Three older women clad in black robes from head to toe, sat on a bench made for them and watched the procedures with a satisfied smile.

Men were busy cooking lizard meat in underground ovens. One of them lifted his gaze over the shallow pit, and Bali's skin tingled. Kamnon. His ochre sarong left his glistening torso bare, where a necklace made of shark teeth rested and tribal tattoos encircled his biceps. The handsome redhead towered over the russet-skinned men tending the fire. Her gaze drifted to his sarong, wondering if the shark wound on his left leg was as deep as rumored. Some said the skin beneath his sarong was as white as the sand.

One of the dark-clad women scowled at him and the rest followed. Tradition-breaker, he was called. He had shirked his duty and not participated in the past season's mating rituals when his mother became a soul wanderer.

He rushed to Bali's side. "Here, let me help you."

"No, it's my right to take it to the pit." Her taut muscles were sore, but she had to end what she had started.

"Will you let me cook it for you?"

She glanced at the other huntresses, wondering if he'd offered for them as well. By their expressions of surprise, Bali knew she was the first. The older women—gnarled hands over their canes—stoically glanced her way.

The Child of Gaia had requested Bali to consider him. And by Gaia she would.

"You might," Bali said with a graceful nod of her head.

Kamnon placed a hand over his chest and smiled. Perhaps he'd asked merely to stop the rumors of breaking tradition so the Islanders would accept him as one of their own.

Bali didn't care why. She allowed herself to smile as she finished dragging the lizard to the pit. The first season of the Cycle had been quite successful to her eyes.

The older women nodded, then glanced at the other huntresses, as if expecting Kamnon to ask another. Kamnon did not.

**

Bali took an aromatic bath so her skin would smell of jasmine. Once she was dry, she crushed oyster shells to make her skin sparkle. Kamnon would be hers tonight under the stars, on this first day of the Cycle's second season.

Her long crimson skirt opened to show her leg. She donned a white cloth, wrapping it around her breasts, but leaving her shoulders and midriff bare.

Her skin was afire. This was the season to love. To kiss and to touch.

Leaving the hut she shared with her mother, Bali strode through the village, her dark hair in loose waves, in tune with the happy season. Drumbeats mixed with men's resonant voices, while the sweet smell of jasmine hung in the air. Violet-blue jacaranda flowers littered the ground in a soft, colorful carpet and blooms brightened the trees. Children ran around and women danced to the rhythm of drums; a couple of the men chanted and thumped their hands on the deerskin instruments.

At a beat change, the women lifted their hands to Gaia, honoring Her, before resuming their dance. It was the only time when Gaia showed Herself next to Helios, shining brightly on the sky, for Islanders to celebrate Her season.

Bali had always loved Her blues and greens. It reminded her of Kamnon's eyes.

Sitting on their bench, the older women of the village watched the dance with joyous expressions, canes carelessly thrown onto the ground, their feet thumping at the drums' beat. A young man offered Bali wine, and with a coy smile she took the clay mug and walked away.

She hummed a lovers' tune while her eyes darted to Gaia, dominating the azure sky. "Oh, Gaia," she whispered as she offered the wine to Her, bells tinkling on her lizard-skin belt and wrists, "let me enjoy this wondrous season. Let Helios shine on me and bless this land. Let Kamnon be mine and only mine."

Gaia seemed to flicker and Bali held her breath, realizing what she'd just asked. Her heart beat fast. Would Gaia be offended if Kamnon remained only with Bali in this second season of the Cycle? Was Bali wrong to want him for herself exclusively? Breaking tradition would be selfish, and she would not want to bring Gaia's displeasure on her.

And yet, having Kamnon for herself was all she wanted.

Gaia looked the same as always, blue and green swirling beneath white clouds.

"Bali!"

And there he was. Smiling, all muscles and tan skin and firm chest. He would be hers. Only hers. Bali's heart skipped a beat and she let herself be caught in the music, her hips responding to the melody. Kamnon approached, clasped her wrist, and made her twirl.

She offered him the mug of wine and he drank slowly, not taking his eyes off her. He set down the cup and placed a crown of jasmine on her hair. She laughed, glad he had noticed how much she loved those flowers.

Shimmying her hips to the chants, she stroked a finger along his jaw, red and blond bristles prickling her. His eyes sparkled and he pulled her to him. She felt the heat from his body, infusing her own.

"Would you choose me and be mine?" he recited as tradition dictated.

"Always," she whispered, tilting her head back and losing herself in his unfathomable eyes.

He lifted her chin. "Always?"

She blushed, realizing what she'd said.

Kamnon bent and brushed his lips against her ear. "I would like that very much."

Her heart light, she glanced at the dark-clad women who were trying hard not to look their way. One woman scowled at her. But it wasn't Bali's fault Kamnon had taken an interest only in her and had played deaf to the older women's scolding. She pressed her mulberry-tinted lips to his, then sighed, content. Her fingers caressed his, with the promise of more. A warm tingle covered her body and their gazes locked as her fingertips relished a last touch.

Kamnon caught her wrist in his gentle grasp and her lips parted expectantly. He had signaled he would not choose any other.

Bali let herself be guided to his hut. She lifted her eyes to Gaia and mouthed her gratitude. Perhaps he might not be hers always, but he would for the rest of the second season.

**

Bali knew the third season of the Cycle had arrived the moment she opened her eyes, gloom in her thoughts a brief fog in her heart. The second season had been to love, and she had loved Kamnon every single moment of it. The new season was to grieve and mourn. Thus, she had left his hut the night before, sadness piercing her heart.

A chill lingered in the air, and she shivered. Her foolishness at not accepting tradition, and the change, had made her sleep with only a thin cotton sheet instead of a sheep-wool blanket. It was inevitable the third season drained away the joy. She put on slippers and donned clothes suited for the colder weather. She combed her hair into three thick braids and secured them atop her head. No kohl for her eyes, no mulberry for her lips, no scented oil for her skin.

Dragging her feet over the reed-covered floor, she reached the cold hearth where Mother was already eating. Pale yellowed light filtered through the windows. No more jasmine in the air.

"Come, breakfast's ready," Mother said. "After you finish, go to the lizards' cave; I've already filled the basket with the rodents, and they're skittish."

"Yes, Mother."

Bali sat and dipped her fork into the smoked fish, wishing for lizard broth or roasted wild boar instead, but there would be no fire in this season. "Kamnon is going fishing today and promised to share his catch." She blushed.

"That boy doesn't respect traditions. Fishing in this season!" Mother held a fist next to her half-eaten cheese. "The Cycle needs to be respected, even by Gaia's children. We will consume what we harvested from the past season, nothing more."

Bali clenched her fists and decided not to finish her meager breakfast. *Who wanted to eat in such a gloomy atmosphere, anyway?*

Leaving her mother, she dashed out with the wicker basket, secured to avoid letting the rodents out. Yesterday's clear skies had given way to deep violet clouds and the light had turned somber. Somber, like her mood.

The lizards' cave was even darker, and she tread carefully on the gray, cold ground, holding the basket close to her body. The small lizards had their spiked tails wrapped around their bodies and would not come out during this season. Lizards did not like the soul wanderers who would visit the Island, but once the new season arrived, they would return to the grasslands beneath the hills and grow fat and huge, ready for the Islanders to hunt them down. As did everyone on the Isle of Veralius, they too respected the Cycle.

Tradition was all that mattered.

She knelt and left the wicker basket full of rodents next to their prostrate forms. Some lifted their heads, their forked tongues slipping in and out, tasting the air.

"Please, accept this offering," she said, her head low, then opened the lid toward them and scuttled away.

On her way back to her hut, she ran into Kamnon.

He reached for her hand. "Bali, I've missed you. My bed felt cold last night."

"I missed you, too." Bali sat on a rock and patted it for him to sit next to her. Trees gave shade, and a cold wind whistled through the leaves.

"We'll be together again before you know it." He plucked a couple of withering flowers and entwined them in Bali's dark hair, his bright smile a contrast against the moody atmosphere.

"How I wish we could." She sighed and laced her fingers with his, feeling the roughness of his palm.

He bumped her shoulder with his. "We could. If you wanted to."

Could they? The stern expressions of the wise women and her mother's scolding came to mind.

"No." Bali shook the flowers from her head. "We need to mourn our dead, and tears should stain our cheeks."

He nodded. "For ghosts to come alive and not forget us."

"For them to relish their memories," Bali recited. "But they are not to see the joy they left behind—"

"—for they might never depart this land," Kamnon added his voice to Bali's.

"Yes. We must honor the Cycle. Every year until we grow old."

Kamnon slapped his hands—those beautiful, callused hands—on his thighs and rose to his feet. "I guess we should. But"—he glanced up to the stormy sky—"she's not watching. Perhaps we could go to my hut."

"No!"

Mother was right. They had to respect tradition and honor Gaia. She would not spill tears over heated rocks when Kamnon chose his second.

"Bali, I know traditions are important." He looked thoughtful. "But should they matter when our hearts are as entwined as ours? I feel like a fish caught in a net when I look into your dark eyes."

"Yes, traditions matter, Kamnon. They define us." She gave him a soft kiss. "I'll see you at the cemetery later."

Her quick steps took her to the rocky beach. Orange petals covered the brick path from the sea to the pantheon, a beacon for the lost souls to find their loved ones. Helios' rays tried to pierce the thick layer of clouds, but they would not touch the faces of the Islanders, not during the season that belonged to the dead.

Glowing orbs lined the path to guide the soul wanderers. Once they found the path of orange petals, they would come from whence they resided during the rest of the Cycle, and the Islanders would mourn, spill their tears onto the ground.

Bali sat on her usual rock, a flat stone that dampened her skirt, the one she had perched upon every first day of this Cycle.

Kamnon's lovemaking was all she wanted, the endless dance that had lasted, and would last, for eternity. But soul wanderers were not allowed to see the mighty creation of a new life. Bali pressed her tawny hands on her covered belly, hoping for a new life, a new soul that would praise and love Gaia.

She knew their offspring would have her black hair and his blue green eyes, maybe his beautiful hands, those hands that handled nets and threw spears. Alas, last season was the only chance she'd have. Islanders could choose a new mate every Cycle or remain with their old, but Gaia's child could not—should not—stay with only one.

In the last Cycle, Kamnon's mother Turia had left the Island as a soul wanderer. Kamnon had fallen into a depression, thus neglecting his duty to partake in the mating rituals.

Turia's eyes had always drifted to the ocean, a longing trapped in her chest that no one could ease. She would stand for hours, sighing, and sometimes crying. The wise women had nodded, knowing Turia longed to return to Primanus where she had conceived Kamnon.

Bali rested her chin on her raised knees and watched the steely ocean, the cold breeze ruffling the delicate strands of her dark hair.

There was nothing she wanted more than to have his love growing in her belly, allowing them to move to their own hut until the baby was born. Then moving to the Gaia hut, where all children grew among the women. Eventually, she and her offspring would have their own hut, just like she and Mother.

Kamnon would take to the sea to fish for every Islander, not only because he liked to do so, but because it reminded him of his mother's love of the ocean.

A strange sadness seized her when she thought of him moving out so quickly once the baby was born, but she dismissed it.

Oh, how silly was she acting!

She glanced up at the cloudy sky, wiping away her absurd tears. There was no one she would rather have, but tradition dictated she had to let him go.

Gaia was hidden now and would reappear when the skies cleared entirely in the last season of the Cycle. When the ghosts of past lives could stroll on the Isle to their souls' content, Helios would cast his golden shining rays on the Isle of Veralius again.

The sky suddenly cleared in one spot and Gaia smiled down at her.

Bali sprang to her feet. The air before her shimmered and mirrored her surprised face. She gasped and threw a hand up to touch the dark hair and tawny skin. It felt cold, hard, like water trapped in a smooth rock. Strange pictures flashed, obscuring her reflection, and she scrambled behind the rock, her arms shaking.

The Portal to Primanus!

Images of a strange village made of glass bewildered her. Instead of simple huts, these constructions were piled one over another, even two or three times five, and their polished surface reflected the sky and a nearby body of water. Oddly dressed people walked too fast, not talking to each other, their eyes focused on shiny rectangles held in their hands or pressed against their ears. A myriad of sounds reached her ears, strident, loud, incomprehensible yet delightful.

Her feet tingled and her body leaned forward, but she didn't abandon her spot behind the rock. Legends of old talked about the strangeness of Primanus, though nothing had prepared Bali for this.

Twenty tens of people rushed past in that strange village and Bali brought a hand to her chest. How was this possible? And yet, there they were, people with pale skin, some with skin darker than the Islanders, and one man sported—Bali cocked her head. Blue hair? How was that possible? The man had the most unusual hair, as bright as a flower, and he was dressed in odd black-and-white robes that didn't look like any sarong but were wrapped around his legs and torso. He glanced up from his shiny rectangle.

His lips parted and he stared at her. "Who are you?" The words were alien, yet she understood them.

"Bali," she whispered, slowly approaching the portal.

Awed, he extended a hand toward her, his fingers touching the silvery screen interposed between them. He was so close, and she only needed to reach out to take his hand. Heart thundering wildly, she stepped even closer. The remote village beckoned her.

"What is this place?" she murmured, aghast.

He turned around. "This? Manhattan."

"What strange words come from your mouth!"

He looked beyond her. "And what's the name of your place?"

"Isle of Veralius."

The blue-haired man took a step back, then glanced around in confusion. "Never heard of it."

She touched the surface, the door to the strange Manhattan, and knew she had to go through. Wasn't that what she was supposed to do? Gulping, she took a step back.

The air shimmered once more and the sea replaced the strange village. The rough steel-gray ocean, nothing more. Gaia flickered once more before thick clouds covered Her, and Bali felt goosebumps.

Guilt. A nauseous feeling in her belly that let her know she'd been wrong to refuse.

Turia had answered the call. Bali had not.

She sat on the rock and brought her knees to her chin.

The children of Gaia were entirely unlike the Islanders. Some had darker skin or strange wheat hair, some, like Kamnon, were white-skinned, just like the humans in those images. Except no child of Gaia had been born with blue hair.

Bali had been chosen to be the carrier of a Gaia child and she had refused. Would she be punished for not answering the call? Worse, the portal had awakened a yearning within her. To visit that magnificent place and see how many people could live in there.

She touched her belly and knew she wouldn't bear Kamnon's child. Gaia wouldn't have beckoned her to Primanus otherwise. Sadness muted her yearning and battled within her like a fierce storm.

Lightning flashed over the ocean and the wind increased. She pushed away strands of hair lashing at her face. Fog appeared and thickened in seconds.

It was time to greet the dead.

Kamnon waited for her beyond the line of trees. Had he seen the portal? But his smile cleared her doubt. And then, she knew: Gaia had tried to take her away from him.

"I'm sorry," he said as he reached for her. "I shouldn't have asked you to break tradition. I know how much you care about that."

She glanced behind her, the portal clear in her mind.

"But... will you stay with me even after we have our first child?" he asked.

Our first.

She buried her face against his bare chest. "That is also against tradition."

He sighed. "Could we find a way?"

The village Manhattan appeared in her thoughts. The noise, the unique garments, and the blue-haired man. What would happen if Gaia opened the portal again? She couldn't give Kamnon a promise she might not keep.

"Let's not think about that. Soul wanderers will arrive tonight."

**

Kamnon held her close, her head resting on his bare shoulder, finally together after the soul wanderers roamed the Isle, during the fourth and final season of the Cycle.

They were in his hut, a small, one-room place, nothing at all like that strange glass village, which seemed so big, so different from here. The images swirled in her head and infused a longing in her chest, a longing she was unable to dismiss. She placed a hand on Kamnon's chest and shifted.

"Have you ever wondered where your father is?" she asked. "Where he was from?"

"No. My mother never talked about him."

"Didn't she say where she went when she answered to Gaia?"

Kamnon removed her hand and stood. She wondered if she could stop loving him.

He drank from the clay jar he kept in one corner. "She was always sad when I asked, so I eventually stopped."

Would Bali be sad too if she were to go to marvelous Manhattan and return? Would she miss that place and its wonders and wallow in despair? She stood and donned her skirt and blouse. It was no use asking herself that.

"Bali."

She stopped. She hadn't realized her feet had taken her to the door.

"Would you stay with me?"

She avoided his gaze. "I have to tend Mother's garden. Wild boars trampled it yesterday."

"You know what I'm asking." He extended his hand toward her. His beautiful, rugged hand.

"I... I will see you tonight."

Bali rushed out of the cabin. Azure reigned in the sky. Blue, like that strange man's hair.

She kept wondering about that shiny rectangle those people seemed to love so much. How could buildings reflect the sky? And what were those peculiar strident sounds?

Now, she would never know, and that nagged at her. Every day.

There might be many Islands. When the souls finally chose to leave, they traveled to Primanus. Turia had met an angel with hair as red as Kamnon's. Perhaps that was why she could not talk about Kamnon's father.

Bali brushed her fingertips over her belly as her bare feet kissed the sand, not sure if she was sad or not that she hadn't conceived a child with Kamnon. She always thought about the possibility of becoming the mother of a Gaia's child. Surely Gaia had not allowed her to have a child with Kamnon because she was fated otherwise. He was devastated, though. And today he had asked her yet once again.

Her steps took her to the ocean, to her usual spot.

The air shimmered and flattened before her. With cautious steps, Bali approached the portal and touched its polished surface. Cold. Instead of the marvelous city she'd dreamed about for the past Cycle, all she saw was her reflection. Her dark hair framing her surprised face at being offered a second chance.

She pressed her palm to the sticky mirror and the mirror reflected not her hand, but one with long, masculine fingers. She was not touching the portal, but a man's hand. The blue-haired man. Primanus shimmered behind him. Magical, mystical.

"You're so beautiful," he whispered, and his fingers entwined her own. "I've dreamed of you for months. Come through."

His fingers closed around hers and she felt him pull, but she remained in her spot. Yes, that must be heaven and the man a beautiful angel and Gaia wanted her to go. And yet, and yet...

"Bali!" came Kamnon's distressed call.

She whipped her head around toward the tree line, and there he was. His face showed despair, yet he remained still. He wouldn't rush her decision. Sadness tugged at his face, knowing she would leave.

And she had to. Not just because of her longing but because it was her duty, wasn't it so?

The blue-haired angel pulled at her; the glass village beckoned.

But she would not hunt lizards in the next season, nor mourn her dead when the soul wanderers came, and she would not have Kamnon by her side and would miss her chance to have a child with him.

A beautiful blue-green eyed child with black hair and strong hands who would learn to be a fisherman.

She recovered her hand and stepped back. "No, I'll stay here."

The blue-haired angel frowned. "Why would you? I saw your Island in my dreams. There's nothing there."

She glanced at Kamnon. "Yes, there is."

Not waiting to see what would happen to the strange village and the angel, she lifted her skirt and ran to Kamnon, who stretched his hand toward her. Happiness replaced his grim expression. She no longer doubted she wanted to stay with him.

She was shown something wonderful, but she had wonderful already.

Burying her face in his chest, Bali felt his arms close tight around her.

"Ask me again," she whispered.

"Will you stay with me?"

"Always."

Ligia de Wit

Ligia de Wit is a bilingual fantasy writer who is an eternal romantic. This led to penning "Always", a story about love and strange lands where anything can happen. When not concocting stories, she works at a global leading distributor company. You can find her at ligiadewit.com[1].

---

1. https://www.ligiadewit.com

Parallel

Avily Jerome

Puffs of dust rose from the thick carpet with every step Jo took. The beam from her flashlight danced across the rich furniture that looked like it had been dropped straight out of the 1800s into the room. Except for the thick layer of dust, everything was in perfect condition.

How had this place not been looted? There was always someone willing to brave the swamps, ticks, and ghosts for a chance at treasure. Intact mansions simply didn't exist.

Except this one.

Well, their loss was her gain. What would this place be like when it was restored? A plantation mansion with original furnishings would be a historic treasure of unparalleled worth.

A draft rustled her hair and a sensation like cold fingers brushed against her arm. She shuddered. No wonder rumors of ghosts in this place were so prevalent.

Documentation was hard to find, and every story was at least second- or third-hand. They said people went in and never came out. Vandals who tried to break windows were chased off by spirits who protected the house. All the usual scary tales that surrounded places like this, but with none of the telltale vandalism that contradicted the narrative. Given the condition of the place, she could almost believe benevolent forces protected it. Even time and weather hadn't done much to damage it.

She brushed the dust from a portrait on the wall. A young belle, smiling, with a mischievous twinkle in her eye, gazed down at her.

Who had the girl been? Had she survived the war? Married an officer, perhaps? Had she been forced to abandon her beautiful home, or had she died young, still as beautiful as she was in the portrait?

History on the mansion was vague, at best. No records of the original owners had survived. She'd come across numerous news articles about people who had said they were going exploring in this area and never returned, but very little about anyone who actually knew anything.

Perhaps she could find some information on the belle somewhere in the house, and use that to jumpstart her search.

The portrait was stunning, and even if she couldn't find any documentation, the mysterious woman's image would be the focal point of the exhibit when Jo made the house into a museum.

She continued around the room, noting the artifacts and looking for clues about the family that had lived there. Ornate candlesticks stood on the mantle. Heavy drapes, free from decay or destruction by moths, hung from the windows. A settee and a finely carved rocking chair sat before the empty fireplace. But nothing gave her any indication of the identity of the inhabitants.

A family Bible would have all the generational information in the front. Where would they have kept something like that?

The draft chilled her again, blowing past her and rustling the pages of an open book on a table opposite the portrait. She walked toward it.

A huge Bible.

It was almost as if a ghost had pointed her to exactly what she was looking for. She touched the pages tenderly, carefully opening to the front page, where the generations would be listed.

The ink was faded and smudged, and in the dim light of the room, even with her flashlight, it was impossible to make anything out. She would have to take this to someone who could preserve it. She sighed wistfully. So much history here, within these pages, within this room.

Above the table with the Bible, an ornate mirror hung from the wall. In it, she could see the reflection of the portrait, dimly illuminated by her flashlight. The girl in the portrait winked at her.

Jo gasped and whirled around, shining her light full on the portrait. The portrait smiled down at her, perfectly still.

The wind from the draft blew by her again, kicking up a swirl of dust and carrying it to the hallway. Jo could almost hear it whisper to her. *This way.*

She followed the eddying dust down the hall and through a pair of wide double doors into a ballroom. Crystal chandeliers hung from the ceiling, catching the fragments of light filtering in and sending it back to her in a shower of prisms. In the far-right corner sat a piano, and behind it, on the right side of the room, a small stage. A mirror took up most of the wall to her left, while the wall straight in front was lined with heavily draped windows.

What would this room look like with the chandeliers lit, with couples twirling across the floor, coming in and out the French doors opening out into the garden where lovers walked? She could almost see the scene reflected in the huge mirror.

No, not almost.

She *could* see it. Ethereal figures danced in the glass. Maybe there really were ghosts here, reliving the days before the war.

Jo walked toward the mirror where the dancers faded in and out of the real reflection, that of the dim, dusty room. The girl from the portrait walked toward her from the other side of the mirror, looking for all the world like she was about to speak.

Jo reached out to touch the glass.

It...rippled. Like the surface of a lake, the glass shimmered under her fingers.

The girl from the portrait reached out and pulled her through, laughing. "Come on in. There are to be soldiers here tonight. Officers, even! Is that all the tighter you can get your corset? Well, you'd best not eat too much, then."

Jo looked down. Had she always been wearing this dress?

Of course she had. What else would she wear to a ball? Besides, blue always was her best color. Her friend was right about the corset, though. Perhaps one of the slaves could get it a bit tighter.

"Rose, why don't you two go to the front hall with your father and greet our guests," a woman who looked like an older version of the girl from the portrait suggested.

"Yes, Mother," Rose, the portrait girl, said. She took Jo's hand and led her out to the front hall.

A man with an oiled mustache and wearing an immaculate suit stood at the doorway. He had Rose's merry, twinkling eyes. He beamed when Rose and Jo walked toward him. "Rose, you certainly are a picture," Rose's father said. He smiled indulgently before glancing over to Jo. "You look lovely, too."

Jo curtsied. Somehow, the movement felt awkward, like she was out of practice, but she smiled and took her place next to Rose.

A sickly looking man and a stout woman made their way up the steps.

"Mr. and Mrs. Warner. So good of you to join us. Do come in," Rose's father said.

Rose curtsied and simpered. "How do you do."

Jo did the same.

In pairs or small groups, more guests filtered in. A group of young men in uniform came in. One by one, they bowed deeply before first Rose, then Jo, before marching proudly to the ballroom.

Rose giggled, her face as bright red as her namesake. "There's a husband there for one of us, mark my words."

A lively jig started in the other room. The sounds of music and laughing and feet tapping floated out.

"Come on, we've played hostess long enough," Rose said. She pranced back to the ballroom, Jo following closely behind.

Rose surveyed the room when they entered, her smile landing on every young man in sight. They all bowed when they caught her eye.

Jo pushed aside a twinge of jealousy and followed the nod of Rose's head. "There. Charles Barrington. He's a little older than you, but he's rich, and rumor has it he stopped courting Frannie Devonshire when she lost weight after her illness and her bosom shrank. He's coming toward you. Smile."

Jo smiled and curtsied as Charles Barrington asked for a dance.

She twirled around the room with him all evening, until Rose pulled her away and forced her into the arms of a soldier, saying, "You have to show him he's not your only option if you want him to commit."

Jo laughed and flirted, danced and ate. Something nagged at the back of her mind, a hint of a memory that she couldn't quite place. A different life, almost like a dream she was waiting to get back to. She pushed the feeling aside and danced until her feet hurt. Finally, when she could barely breathe, she excused herself and wandered down the hall toward the parlor. She sat in the rocking chair in the dark, quiet room, glancing absently at the mirror above the Bible. The room looked different in the reflection. Older, somehow.

A woman with a small, oddly shaped candle entered the room, her footsteps sending puffs of dust into the air. Jo stood and turned around, scanning the room for the intruder, but no one was there.

She looked back in the mirror. The woman was still there, in the reflection. She was dressed strangely, in trousers and a blue shirt that looked like it was designed for a man, except that it exposed the top of her full bosom.

She looked familiar, but Jo couldn't place why.

The half-formed memory tugged at her. The woman in the mirror was looking for the Bible. She couldn't say how she knew; she just knew.

Jo walked to the table and touched the pages of the Bible. The woman in the mirror came toward her. Jo looked at the woman and she stared back for a long time, but the other woman didn't seem to see Jo.

"There you are." Rose's voice broke the silence. "Charles is looking for you. Come on."

"I'll be there in a moment." Jo looked back at the woman in the mirror, but all she saw was herself, dressed in those strange clothes. She looked down at her ball gown. No, these were the strange clothes. That girl out there, that was who she was supposed to be. She reached toward her reflection, trying to join it on the other side, but it didn't see her.

What was she doing there? No, what was she doing *here*?

A confused jumble of memories ricocheted around her mind. She didn't belong here with Rose. She belonged out there, exploring, researching, documenting.

"Hurry up, Jo!" Rose called.

She had come through the mirror in the ballroom. Maybe if she could get her reflection back there, she could get out. "I'm coming," she called back.

She went to the mirror and shouted at her reflection. "This way!"

She ran back toward the ballroom and stopped in front of the mirror, searching for her true reflection.

It wasn't there. The mirror was solid, not rippling when she touched it like it had when she came in the first time.

Rose came up beside her and grabbed her hand. From the corner of her eye, Jo saw the reflection walk toward the mirror. The mirror rippled.

Jo reached for the mirror.

She started to step through, back into her reflection.

###

The girl from the portrait reached out and pulled her through, laughing. "Come on in. Where have you been? You'll be lucky if you don't get whipped. Where is your uniform?"

Jo looked down at her dress. Plain, shapeless, faded blue, but the nicest one she owned.

A man with a drooping mustache approached them, wearing fine livery. "Quickly, Rose," he hissed. "They're waiting." He glared at Rose, then turned his attention to Jo. "Where is your uniform? No time for it now, you must hurry."

Jo thought the man was Rose's father, but she wasn't sure how she knew, and she didn't have a chance to think about it.

Rose pulled her along to the other end of the room where a servant's door opened up into a dim hallway. The hallway led to the kitchen, where several other servants scurried around, making food and arranging it on trays.

Someone thrust a tray into her hands and shoved her back toward the hallway. She followed Rose back out into the ballroom where guests were beginning to arrive.

A tall, attractive black man in an officer's uniform smiled broadly at the guests pouring in. "Welcome," he smiled, shaking the hands of those sweeping in.

Something felt... backwards. It took Jo several moments to realize what it was. All the guests—the soldiers in their freshly pressed uniforms, the belles in their extravagant gowns, the dowagers with their disapproving glares—they were all black.

Is this how it should have been? Jo wondered. Maybe. *But it's not how it was.*

The thought trampled through her mind and skittered away before she had time to latch onto it.

A girl in a blue gown with at least a dozen petticoats danced toward Jo and sampled some of what was on Jo's tray. Her dark eyes raked Jo from top to bottom. "Where's your uniform? Father is going to be so angry."

She danced away again with a little laugh.

The officer who'd been greeting guests noticed her at that moment. A much younger man stood by his side, looking nervous.

I know him.

The thought tried to dance away, but she grabbed onto it. *I know him. His name is Tim. I saw him... in a news article.*

A news article? When had she ever read a news article? Could she even read?

The officer and Tim marched toward her, and her thoughts centered on them, pushing away the memory of the news article.

"Where is your uniform?" the officer demanded.

"I—I'm not sure," Jo stammered.

The officer frowned and turned to Tim. "Well, lad, come on. If you're going to marry my daughter and take over my estate, you need to get used to this."

Tim looked uncomfortable. Confused.

The officer snatched the tray from Jo's hands and thrust it at another servant, then grabbed her by the arm, dragging her down another servant's hallway to a dank, windowless storage room.

He shoved Jo to the ground and pressed his foot into her back, between her shoulder blades.

"Go on then, grab the whip."

Jo raised her head to see Tim reach tentatively for a whip that hung from two nails on the wall. He glanced at the officer, whose face she couldn't see, then slowly raised the whip, bringing it down in a half-hearted swat at her backside.

"No, son, like this." The officer took the whip and moved his foot. The whip whistled through the stale air and lashed against her back.

Jo screamed and tried to roll away, but the officer stepped on her arm, crushing it beneath his weight, and handed the whip back to Tim.

"Try again, son," the officer said.

Tim raised the whip again.

"Tim, no! Stop!" Jo screamed.

Tim took a step back, shock written across his features.

"How do you…"

The officer grabbed the whip and raised it.

"You're not supposed to be here," Jo cried.

The whip landed again.

"You're stuck. We both are," she gasped between lashes.

Tim glanced uncertainly between Jo and the officer, as the whip came down again.

"Help me!" Jo begged.

In a sudden rush, Tim rammed his shoulder into the officer's torso, knocking him backward off her arm, grabbed Jo by her other arm, and hauled her to her feet. He ran out into the hallway, through a maze of servant's corridors, until they found themselves in a parlor.

A portrait of a woman sat above the mantle. It was the young woman who'd told her that her father would be angry that she wasn't wearing her uniform. But something wasn't right. Had she been in this room before? Something told her she had, and that the portrait was different than it had been before, but she couldn't quite remember how it was.

"We have to get out of here." Tim's voice interrupted her thoughts.

Across the room, the family Bible sat displayed on a table. There was something about that Bible, something important.

Ignoring Tim, she walked toward it. Above it, a mirror reflected the room. Reflected the portrait. But the image in the portrait was not the officer's daughter, it was another woman.

Rose.

Why was Rose's picture in this house?

She took another step and saw her own reflection—except it wasn't her, either.

"He's coming!" Tim hissed.

Jo grabbed his hand and raced out into the hallway. She thought she knew which way the front door was from here. "This way!" she said.

But instead of finding the front door, she found the door to the ballroom, with its wall of mirrors. In the mirror, she saw the reflection of herself that wasn't quite herself, the same one she'd seen in the parlor, and reached for it.

The girl from the portrait reached out and pulled her through, laughing. "Come on in. There are to be soldiers here tonight. Officers, even! Is that what you're wearing? You'll get blood all over it."

Jo looked down.

The dress she wore was in a style that felt unfamiliar, and yet she knew it was the correct fashion for a High Ritual. But she had only been an observer before, not a participant. Was she supposed to actually perform the ritual?

Her back was sore, as though she'd scraped it on barbed wire or something. When had that happened? Her arm was sore, too, but she couldn't quite figure out why.

She looked at her friend, clothed in a white, shapeless tunic.

A man in a similar tunic with a hood covering his head and obscuring his face walked toward them. "Rose, I thought you said your friend would be performing the ritual tonight."

Though she couldn't see his eyes, she could feel the disapproval in his gaze.

"It will be fine, Father," Rose smiled. "She just wanted to look nice. This is a momentous occasion."

Rose pulled Jo's hand and led her toward the stage at the back of the room where a table was set up.

Jo swallowed, her heartrate jumping at the sight. It wasn't just a table, it was a gurney, with leather straps to tie something down hanging from the sides. Beneath the table was a trough.

What was she supposed to do? She couldn't remember, and yet she knew that the consequences of failure would be terrible.

Rose nudged her into position behind the gurney, where she'd be visible to everyone in the room. More and more people crowded inside, all wearing the same shapeless white gowns that Rose and her father wore, some of them with hoods, others with their faces showing.

Her eyes locked with a man toward the back of the room.

She knew him. Where did she know him from? His dark eyes looked afraid as he stared at her.

Tim. His name was Tim. Why did she know his name? Why was he here?

Someone screamed, and Rose turned her attention to the door to the servant's hallway, where Rose's father and another man wearing a similar hood dragged a woman into the room.

Jo recognized the woman, and a sense of distant familiarity washed over her. The woman was in her mid-forties, but looked much older, with her pale skin that sagged and wrinkled around her eyes and her blonde hair that was streaked heavily with gray.

Jo had seen her on a website. What was a website? Where had Jo heard that term, and what did it mean? She couldn't quite remember, but she knew it to be true. She'd seen the woman on a website when she was doing research. The woman—Carly—was a historian. She'd written numerous articles about Southern history. She was working on a book about forgotten people and places, and she'd talked about visiting an old plantation rumored to be hidden deep in the swampy forest in southeastern Louisiana.

Was this Louisiana? Was this the plantation Carly was looking for?

Rose's father and the other man dragged Carly to the gurney and forced her onto it, strapping her arms and legs down.

Carly looked at Jo, tears streaming down her face and into her hair and ears. "Help me."

Jo looked around. Could she? Even if she could get the straps undone, she could never fight off this many people and get out the door. But she had to try.

Rose's father turned to face the gathered crowd.

Jo reached toward one of the straps that held down Carly's arms. Maybe, if their attention was focused on him, they wouldn't notice.

"Thank you for coming," Rose's father said.

Jo fumbled with the strap.

"The powers that grant us immortality demand a price," Rose's father said. "Those who wish to join us must prove their loyalty by partaking in the sacrifice."

Jo slipped the buckle off the first strap, freeing Carly's left arm. Carly waited, holding very still, as Jo's hands went to the next strap.

"One such initiate will now join us in immortality," he said. He turned and thrust a long, sharp knife with a gilded handle into Jo's hands.

She stared at it for a long moment, unsure what to do.

"Go on, then," he said, indicating Carly's chest, where her flower-patterned brown gown, wet with sweat, shifted with every breath.

Jo hesitated only a moment, then sliced through the second strap holding Carly down. Carly sat up and reached for the strap around her ankles while Jo raised the knife to ward off Rose's father, who stepped toward her.

"You are not worthy," he sneered. He lunged for the knife and grabbed it from her hand before she had time to react, slashing her fingers in the process.

Jo clenched her fist, but several drops of blood spattered from her hand, splashing on her gown.

Slamming his fist into Carly's chest, Rose's father pinned her back down on the gurney and lifted the knife.

Carly's scream was cut short as the knife plunged into her heart.

Jo choked and stumbled backward. The crowd cheered, and in the brief moment when all their attention was on the bloody knife squelching as it pulled away from Carly's flesh, Jo broke for the door on the other end of the room, shoving past the startled people in their white gowns.

The man at the back, Tim, pushed past those near him and ran toward her.

Was he going to try to stop her?

She dashed into the hallway and glanced both ways, not sure which way to go.

Tim joined her and grabbed her hand. "This way!" he said, starting to pull her toward a large parlor down the hall.

They weren't fast enough.

Rose and her father grabbed Jo from behind and pulled her back into the ballroom.

Jo struggled, writhing to escape their grasp, and fell into one of the large mirrors that lined one wall of the ballroom.

A girl reached out and pulled her through, laughing. "Come on in. You're late."

Late? Late for what?

The girl's eyes raked Jo up and down. "Is that what you're wearing?"

Jo looked down. A blue gown, low-cut and revealing an enormous expanse of bosom, swept the ground in graceful folds around her feet.

"You may get the best price, but remember, the richest ones are often the cruelest."

The way she said that made Jo's skin crawl. Pain flared in her back. Had she hurt it somehow?

She clenched a fist, and that hurt, too. She glanced down to see a freshly healed scar running across her fingers. She had a vague memory of a knife, long and covered with blood.

She blinked and the memory faded.

The girl marched up to where a small stage was set up at the back of the room. A man stood there, lining people up at the edge of the stage.

"I found her, Father," the girl said.

The man glanced over. "Thank you, Rose." He looked Jo up and down. "You warned her about not trying too hard, didn't you?"

Rose shrugged. "I tried, but she wore that anyway."

Rose's father shook his head. "Well, best of luck to you. Come on, then. Get in line. We're about to start." He shoved Jo into place between two others, one a young man, the other a woman a few years older than Jo.

Another woman wearing a brown dress patterned with small pink flowers came out from the side door and surveyed the line of people waiting by the stage. "Are we ready?"

Rose and her father both bowed slightly.

"Yes, Madame," Rose's father said.

"Good, then. You may let them in," the woman said.

Jo recognized her. Where did she know the woman from? Her name was Carly, Jo thought, and she was younger than she appeared.

A crowd filed in from the main doorway to the ballroom and took their places by the mirrors along the opposite wall.

Carly stepped up to a podium on the stage, and waited until the crowd quieted and looked at her expectantly.

"You all know the rules," Carly said. "You all have your room assignments. Highest bidder takes the subject, and you have two hours."

Jo's heart thumped in her chest. That didn't sound very promising.

"Let's begin," Carly said.

Rose's father shoved the first person in line, a girl in her early twenties wearing a simple pink gown, up onto the stage next to Carly.

"Ten, do I have ten?"

A man near the front of the crowd lifted a paddle.

"Ten. Do I have fifteen?"

The girl started to whimper.

A woman with a sadistic sneer on her painted lips raised a paddle.

"Fifteen. Do I have twenty?" Carly asked.

Near the back of the crowd stood a cluster of young people looking confused. Jo stared at them. There was something familiar about them.

She stared, trying to place the memory. They were high school students. They'd posted a selfie on social media just before going camping. That was the last anyone ever saw of them.

Selfie. Social media. Jo knew she should know what those things meant, but her memory was foggy and she couldn't push past the shroud to get at the meaning.

"I've been in this one before," the young woman in line in front of Jo whispered, trembling. "I was purchased by her." She nodded toward the sneering woman with the painted lips and held up a hand. The end of her pinky finger was missing, a faded pink scar all that was left of the spot above the last knuckle. "She did this before I managed to escape and reset."

Reset? What did that mean?

The first girl was purchased by the sneering woman, and the next was shoved onto the stage.

Carly started the bidding.

One by one, the others in line with Jo were auctioned off for their two hours of... what, exactly? Sex? Torture? All of the above?

The young woman in front of Jo went to a man with bored expression.

Rose's father shoved Jo onto the stage, making her stumble toward Carly.

"Do I have ten?" Carly asked.

A man near the front, with gaps in his teeth and an eager glint in his eyes as he stared at Jo's bosom lifted his paddle.

Jo frantically searched the crowd for someone, anyone but him.

Her eyes caught a young man with black skin who looked as confused as she felt. She knew him. She'd seen him more than once.

Tim.

Recognition sparked in Tim's eyes, and a bond of mutual understanding passed between them.

He lifted his paddle.

Jo breathed a sigh of relief. Maybe together they could get out of here.

The first man lifted his paddle, and then Tim raised the bid.

"Thirty," Carly said. "Do I have thirty-five?"

Before anyone could respond, the doors to the ballroom crashed open and an older gentleman burst in.

"The authorities are coming!" the gentleman shouted.

"Get rid of the evidence!" Rose's father said.

Carly led the way into a servant's hallway. Jo followed closely behind, and the others trailed after as they hurried down the dark, narrow space.

Carly opened a door and motioned Jo to go inside.

It was dark. So dark Jo couldn't see beyond the first step that led down into a cavernous room.

Jo paused.

Carly pulled a long, shining knife from her belt and shoved it into Jo's heart.

Warm, wet blood spurted out, soaking Jo's chest and dress as Carly pulled the knife out.

Jo stared at her, her mind going dark.

The last thing she knew was Carly shoving her down the stairs into the blackness.

The girl from the portrait reached out and pulled her through, laughing. "Come on in. There are to be soldiers here tonight. Officers, even! Is that all the tighter you can get your corset? Well, you'd best not eat too much, then."

Avily Jerome

Avily Jerome is a writer and freelance editor. She spent five years as the Editor of *Havok Magazine* (now *Havok Publishing*). Her short stories have been published in multiple magazines and anthologies, both print and digital. She has judged several writing contests, both for short stories and novels, and she is a book reviewer for Lorehaven Magazine. Her novel, *The Breeding*, was a finalist in the 2019 Realm Awards for the Supernatural/Paranormal category as well as Book of the Year, and its sequels, *The Possessing* and *The Haunting*, as well as *Swimmer*, a Little Mermaid-inspired contemporary fantasy novel, are also available.

She loves all things SpecFic and writes across multiple genres. She is also a writing conference teacher and presenter, and she enjoys speaking to local writers' groups and going to SFF cons.

She is a wife and the mom of five kids. She loves living in the desert in Phoenix, AZ, and when she's not writing, she loves reading, spending time with friends, and experimenting with different art forms.

The Devil Made Her Do It

Kaye Lynne Booth

(First published in *Relationship Add Vice* anthology
December 15, 2017, by Zombie Pirates Publishing)

Betty Lou was debugging the new program she'd been working on. She had tried to run it three times now, but each time something went wrong. Now, she thought she'd finally fixed it, worked out all the bugs, so it should run smooth. She hit execute, holding her breath to see what would happen. After thirty seconds, an error message appeared on her screen.

"Dag-nabbit!" she said, shaking a fist at her monitor.

"Problems?" a male voice said from behind her, making her jump in her seat. She was not aware anyone else was there this late in the day. She swiveled her chair around to see a tall, pencil-thin man, dressed all in black, leaning against the cubicle partition behind her. His mahogany-brown hair was pulled back into a ponytail at the back of his neck, revealing a dark-complexioned face with rather sharp features.

She craned her neck to look up into his large brown eyes. "May I help you?" she asked.

"That depends," he replied, curling his mouth at the corners in the hint of a smile. "Are you Miss Dutton?"

"Yes... Betty Lou Dutton," she said. "How can I help you?"

"I'm Jonathon Silk," he said. His smile revealed a mouthful of the whitest teeth she'd ever seen. "I'm a professor at the University and I need a program written to use for my classes. Mr. Crumbly said you were the person to talk to."

"Oh, I see," she said, but in truth she didn't. Mr. Crumbly was a little beetle of a man, who had never even acknowledged her existence up until now. "Did he say why I would be the person for the job?"

"Well, he said you were quite good at what you do," Silk said, scratching the goatee on his long, square chin. "I believe 'quite talented' were his words."

"Really?" Betty Lou said in disbelief. "Mr. Crumbly said that about me?"

"Indeed, he did," he said. "Was he mistaken?" He raised a brow.

"Oh – no. No," she said, straightening her blazer. "I'm sorry. What kind of program is it you need?"

The corners of his mouth turned up once more. "It's quite complicated," he said. "Perhaps I could explain it to you over dinner?"

"I... um, that is..." she mumbled, not knowing what to say. "This is highly unusual."

"Yes, I know, but it's getting late," Silk said. "I didn't want to keep you here after hours. I thought we might grab a bite while we worked. If you think it would be inappropriate..."

"What? Oh, no. I was in the middle of something," Betty Lou said, waving a hand toward her computer, trying to cover up the flustered feeling stirring within her. "But it can wait until tomorrow. I'll just shut this down and grab my purse."

"Fine, then," he said. The gleam of his teeth caught her eye again, as he smiled once more. "I'll wait here."

She turned back to her computer. With a few quick keystrokes she saved her program and shut it down for the night. She wasn't sure what to think about this man. He was handsome in an odd way, not the sort of man she would normally be attracted to. But there was something different about him-a weird sort of magnetism that made her want to go along with his requests, no matter how strange they seemed. "There. Now let me grab my purse and we'll be off," she said, swiveling her chair back around to face him.

He sat on the corner of Julie's desk, in the cubicle behind hers, with his feet crossed at the ankles. "No hurry," he said, raising those gorgeous brown eyes to meet hers.

She went into the break room, taking her purse out of her locker, and made a quick stop in the ladies' room, where she took note of her appearance in the mirror as she washed her hands. Her reflection revealed the perfect picture of a professional woman, her white blouse and dark blue skirt with matching blazer, pressed neatly this morning, with a minimum of wrinkling from the day's wear. With this unscheduled working dinner, Betty Lou was thankful for her practical black pumps. She didn't know how her co-worker, Susan, could stand to work in heels all day. Her straight black hair was drawn back from her face into a tight bun atop her head. She smoothed the spots where stray ends poked out with wet hands before drying, hurrying back to her cubicle. For some reason she didn't understand, she couldn't wait to get out of there.

* * * * *

"Is your shrimp all right?" Silk asked. He sat across the fancy table from her, sipping his glass of wine. The dim lighting softened his features, making him appear too young to be a professor.

Betty Lou dabbed her mouth with her napkin, which was embroidered with the restaurant's logo. "Oh, yes, it's delicious," she replied. "I haven't had a meal like this in... well, in a very long time. Thank you."

"It's the least I can do after I've kept you so long after working hours," he said, giving her that little hint of smile which she was beginning to find very sexy.

"Yes. You know, you still haven't told me about the program you need," she said.

"I haven't, have I?" he said. "I've been having such an enjoyable evening with you, I almost forgot all about it." He set his fork down on his empty plate. "Would you like some more wine?"

"No, thank you," Betty Lou said. "I'm sure I've had enough. I would like to hear about the program." She was finding it difficult after one glass to keep her mind focused on why she was there. She didn't often imbibe, and the alcohol seemed to go right to her head.

"Oh, yes, the program," he said. "Well, it's difficult to explain. You see I want you to devise a program to compile students' information and predict which ones show the most promise based on personal data." Motioning the waiter over, he said, "Care for some dessert?"

"No, thank you," she said. "There are too many variables. A program like that doesn't exist."

"I know. That's why I want you to create it," he replied, pointing a slender forefinger at her. He gave her a wink. "Are you sure you won't have dessert? They have a delicious devil's food cake here. You should try it."

"All right, I'll try it," she said, surprising herself. She'd had no intention of having dessert, but he made it sound so tempting. "So, what kind of data would go into this program? Where would it come from?" she asked.

"Two slices of devil's food cake, please," he said to the waiter. Then to her, he said, "From the student files, of course."

"But I thought all of that information was confidential," she said. "How can you have access to it?"

"No need for you to worry about that, my dear," he said, pausing while the busboy cleared away their dirty plates. When he had gone, Silk continued, "All you need to worry about is making sure the information will get processed correctly, in order to produce accurate results. You can do that, can't you?"

His gaze was direct and a little unsettling. "Well, I don't know," she said, repositioning in her chair. "I've never tried anything like it before. I suppose I could try. What will you do with these results?"

The waiter returned, setting their cakes in front of them. When he had gone, Silk said, "So many questions." He took a bite of cake. When he had swallowed it, he continued, looking right into her eyes, "Let me lay this on the line for you. Your job will be to create the program. You don't need to worry about little things such as what will be done with the results. I'm willing to pay you a good amount of money to write it, without all the questions." He wasn't smiling now. His expression was as serious as death.

"You mean, you'll pay the agency," she said, meeting his stare. "Maybe you should go back to Mr. Crumbly and ask him to suggest someone else for the job. I don't even know if I can create the program you want. Now, if you'll excuse me," she said scooting her chair back.

"Now wait a minute," he said, placing a hand over hers. "I see we've had a misunderstanding. I don't want to hire the agency. I want to hire you. I'm willing to pay quite well for your services, much more than what the agency would pay."

Betty Lou stopped, staring at him in amazement. "You want to hire me?" she asked. "But... Mr. Crumbly..."

"Yes. Yes," he said, patting her hand like she was a child who needed comforting, "Mr. Crumbly was well aware of what I was proposing." He took his hand from hers, reaching into his back pocket, pulling out his wallet. "Now how does a retainer of say, a thousand dollars sound to you?" Slick as snake oil, he produced ten one-hundred-dollar bills, fanning them out as if he were a magician asking her to pick a card.

"I... I don't know what to say," she said, staring in awe at the money he held out before her. It was more than she made in a month. Crumbly knew he was offering her a new job. That's why he had chosen her. Not because she was "talented", but because she was expendable.

"Say yes," he said, inching the money closer to her. "This is just the beginning. I will pay you very well."

In an instant, Betty Lou was angrier with Crumbly than she was wary of this man and his motives. She reached out, taking the money from his hand. "All right, yes," she said.

"Good," said Silk, settling back in his seat again. "Now please, you haven't even tasted your delicious cake." He waved his hand toward her dessert plate, then picked up his fork, taking another bite. "Mmmmm," he said. "This is something you don't want to miss."

* * * * *

Betty Lou was busy trying to work out the latest kink that had occurred with her program. The data John Silk provided from student files had caused the program to malfunction every time for the past two months. She was sure much of it was confidential information he should not have access to, and she knew her program was cracking into places it shouldn't be able to access, like the student financial aid files. She had questioned him about it earlier, when he came home for lunch, but he had brushed it off, telling her not to concern herself.

Her screen flashed another error message. "Fiddlesticks!" she said to the room that now served as her office. She pushed her chair back from the desk, rubbing her temples. She needed a break. She slipped off the shiny black heels John had insisted on buying her, heading barefooted into the kitchen to make a cup of tea.

As she passed through living room, a wisp of hair fell into her line of vision in the mirror off the entry. She would never be able to tolerate wearing her hair down, as John wanted her to. She couldn't stand having hair in her face. She brushed it back, smoothing it into place with her fingers and re-doing the loose ponytail at the back of her neck, which had been her idea of compromise. Still, she looked like a different woman than the one who had taken this job eight months ago.

Loose hair in her face wasn't the only thing that showed transformation. Looking her reflection's image up and down, she wondered who the woman in the mirror was. The one wearing the sheer lace blouse and tight red leather miniskirt that barely covered her butt couldn't possibly be her. Could it? She could not be that woman with the heavily made-up face and false eye lashes. That was not her, but someone Jon Silk wanted her to be; someone he was trying to mold her into.

She supposed it was worth it. In bed the man did things she'd never even imagined, things that drove her wild with desire. So, what if he preferred her to dress in slutty attire? If that was what wound his clock and got that fabulous tongue and huge penis into action, she could tolerate it for a while. Heck, she'd run around the house all night in her birthday suit, in fact, she had when he'd requested her to, and he'd made it worth her while. She thought back on that night, smiling to herself.

A loud pounding on the door made her turn with a start. "FBI! Open up!"

She hurried into the living room, but before she could reach the door, it flew open, smashing against the wall. Several agents burst into the apartment, spreading out in all directions at once.

"What the heck is going on here?" Betty Lou demanded; her China teacup suspended in mid-air.

"We have a warrant to search these premises, Ma'am," the lead agent said, handing her a folded paper.

"Wh... what?" she asked. "Why?"

"We've got a lot of computer equipment back here, sir," an agent said, coming out of the office.

"Be sure you get all of the hard drives," the lead agent replied. "I want them gone over with a fine-tooth comb."

"I don't understand," said Betty Lou, feeling tears well up in her eyes. In fact, she understood more than she wanted to. It appeared she'd let herself be taken in by his suave charm. How could she have been so stupid?

A young blond agent came out of the back bedroom she shared with John. "We're clear. There's no one here but her, sir," he said.

"Damn it!" said the lead agent. "It looks like Silk slipped through our fingers again."

There was a crash as her teacup slipped out of her hand, smashing to the teakwood floor, shattering in a million pieces. She had forgotten she was holding it. Her mind had gone numb.

The lead agent turned back to her. "Where is he, Miss Dutton?"

"Who?"

"Silk. Who else?"

"He's at the University," she said.

The lead agent sighed. "Now Miss Dutton," he said, talking to her as if she were a small child, "he is not at the University. I'm afraid he knows we're onto him. He wouldn't go back there. Now if you can't tell me where he is, I'm afraid you'll have to take the fall alone."

"The fall?" she questioned her hearing. "F... for what? What is it you think John has done?"

"What hasn't he done, Miss Dutton," he said. "I know a bad man when I see one, and he's a B-A-D man. Pilfering from federal funding is nothing to be laughed at. Now, where is he?"

"If he's not at the University, I don't know," she said, her heart sinking down into her stomach, making it feel sour. The agents talked as if Silk had fled. He wouldn't leave her here to deal with this alone, would he? Her sour stomach said he might.

"Okay, if that's the way you want to play it..." the lead agent said, turning to the agent who had come from the bedroom. "Book her."

"Wait. What have I done?" Betty Lou protested.

The blond agent stepped toward her, "Put your hands on the wall and spread your legs," he commanded, turning her toward the wall with a hand on her shoulder. She turned her head to see her reflection in the entry mirror, tears streaming down her face as she tried to do what he said. The tight, faux leather miniskirt made it difficult to get her feet even shoulder width apart.

"You have the right to remain silent..."

The Not So Perfect Prince

By Kaye Lynne Booth

Once upon a time there was a handsome prince, named Geoffry who traveled across the entire kingdom in search of a wife, but he wasn't able to find one woman who he deemed worthy in all the land. For although there were many beautiful and desirable woman within its borders, Prince Geoffry found at least one flaw with each one. Either she had the wrong color hair, or her skin was too dark, or he didn't like the way she walked..., or any number of other traits which he considered to be defects. And when he found such a flaw, he did not hesitate to point them out for all to see, sometimes even ridiculing the poor woman publicly until she ran away in tears. Some even attempted to take their own lives, because they were so overwhelmed by the embarrassment of it, so shamed by his public displays.

Then one day, while searching the mountainside and about giving up on the search, he came across a small cabin hidden deep in the woods. Now Prince Geoffry was weary and desired a place to stop for the night, so he sent his footman, William, to knock on the door and request food and shelter.

A hunchbacked old hag answered the door. She had a pointed nose, so sharp it could put out an eye, and her hair was a dirty gray, hanging over her face in long, stringy lengths, almost down to her knobby knees. "Who are you and what is it you want?" she asked, pointing a boney finger with a sharp tipped nail at him.

"His highness, Prince Geoffry wishes to take rest and nourishment here, Madame," the footman responded, taking a step back to avoid losing the tip of his nose by that nail.

"Of course, of course,'" said the hag, giving a crooked smile which revealed a mouthful of jagged teeth. "I'm willing to provide accommodations for a very reasonable price. Being that he's the Prince and all, I'm willing to offer you a very special deal."

"You wish compensation... from Prince Geoffry?" the footman said with a puzzled expression.

The hag tilted her head to one side, scowling. "Why? He can afford it, can't he?"

Prince Geoffry watched the exchange from atop his mount, but although his father's coffers were brimming over with gold and jewels and he could well afford to pay ten times any price the old hag might ask, the hag's words aggravated him, stirring his ire. He slid down out of his saddle, landing on the ground with a loud thud, and confronted his potential hostess.

"Old woman! What's the matter with you?" he said in a gruff voice. "Do you not pay tribute to your King? How dare you to ask a price from me for your services, you ugly old biddy? Why, I wouldn't sleep in your dirty hovel, anyway. Why don't you go take a bath and clean this place up?"

Instead of begging his pardon from the reprimand as expected, the hag turned and pointed her sharp, boney finger at Prince Geoffry's face, making a small slice across the perfect skin of his cheek.

"Don't you talk to me like that, young man. Prince or not, I'm still your elder," she hissed at him. "Oh, I know you. You have no respect. No respect for your elders... and no respect for women, I hear."

She took a step back and opened her hand, blowing her breath toward him, and with it a magic powder which she held concealed, blowing it right into his face. A puff of smoke surrounded him. "If you're going to act like a toad, you should be one."

The footman stepped forward, and she turned toward him. She blew the remainder of her magic powder on Willliam, followed by a smaller puff of smoke. "Not one word from you, you old goat."

When the smoke cleared, before the hag, where the footman and Prince Geoffry had been, there was now a brown billy goat and a small green frog. The billy goat bleated. The frog croaked.

"I'd pity the girl who had to marry you. Let's see you find a wife now," the hag said to the frog, cackling an evil laugh before going back into her cabin and slamming the door behind her.

The frog hopped over to the Billy goat, who used to be his footman. He ordered the goat to ram the door and get that nasty old hag back out here... or at least, he tried to, but all he could do was to croak rapidly. So, he hopped over and threw himself into the door, hoping that the goat would get the idea. After several attempts, which seemed to result in nothing but a raging headache, his efforts paid off.

The Billy goat rammed the door of the cabin again and again until finally, the hag opened the door again. "What is it?'" she demanded, ignoring the Billy goat and glaring down at the frog. Then she reached down and scooped him up in the palm of her gnarled old hand. "Oh, snail's tails!" she exclaimed. "You're no toad. You're a frog. I'm going to have to work on that spell."

The frog croaked at her again. "Oh relax," she said. "All that really means is that if you could find a girl stupid enough to fall in love with you, she could kiss you to break the spell. A toad would have been irreversible, like the goat."

The goat turned his head in her direction and bleated.

She turned and hissed at him. "You heard me. Irreversible," she said, setting the frog on top of the goat's head, right between his horns. "Now run along. Both of you. Be gone." She clapped her hands, and the billy goat ran off down the path and back into the forest the way they had come.

The billy goat ran and ran. No matter how much the frog croaked for him to stop, he wouldn't. On he ran until he was so tired, he couldn't run anymore.

When he finally stopped, the frog hopped down from the goat's head. He sat there with the goat, who used to be his footman, with the realization that he was really the Prince, but no way to return to his natural form. He sat down next to the goat, pondering his dilemma, and a tiny tear escaped from the corner of his eye and ran down his shiny green cheek.

Just then, a lovely maiden happened down the path with a basket of flowers on her arm. She was skipping and singing a pretty song in the most beautiful voice the frog had ever heard. She was the most beautiful maiden, with long, blonde tresses that hung in ringlets almost to the ground and blue eyes that felt like they could swallow him whole. As soon as he saw her, he knew she was the one who he'd been searching for; he knew it in his heart of hearts. She was perfect.

She skipped right up to the goat. "Hello goat. What are you doing here?" she asked.

The goat bleated. She almost didn't notice the tiny frog sitting next to the goat, but then the frog croaked loud and hopped right up on her shoulder. She gave him a sideways glance, because her eyes were so close to her shoulder that it was the only way of looking at him there without going cross-eyed. "Hello, who are you?" she said, holding out her palm.

The frog croaked, hopping off her shoulder and into her dainty hand. He looked up at her with his big round frog's eyes, trying to figure out how to show her his true identity. She stared back at him, meeting his gaze as if she knew he had something to tell her. Then she saw the tear on his cheek.

"Oh, what's wrong, little guy?" she asked, reaching up and wiping the tear away with her fingertip.

The frog croaked at her once more.

"Aren't you cute," she said, bringing her hand closer, so she could get a better look at him. "If you weren't a frog, I'd marry you."

The frog hopped up and down on her palm in excitement.

"It's okay, little fella," she said, trying to calm him. Then she brought her hand up to her lips and, ever so gently, she placed a kiss on his forehead.

In a big puff of smoke, he became Prince Geoffry once more.

"My Lady, you are perfect," he said, bowing before her with a swoosh of his royal purple cape. "Now that I'm back to myself, we shall be married at once."

The girl backed up a stepped, looking him over. "Aren't you even going to consult me about this?" she said. "What if I don't want to marry you?"

Prince Geoffry froze, staring at her, unable to believe his ears. "Well, of course you want to," he said with a puzzled expression. "After all, I am the perfect Prince. What woman wouldn't want to be my Princess?"

"Any woman with a tad bit of self-respect," she suggested. "I've heard all about you. You are not a kind man." Then she stepped back, shaking her head. "No, I was in love with the frog. As a Prince, you're not so perfect. I'd rather keep the frog. If I kiss you again, will you turn back?"

Prince Geoffry was astounded. He had scoured the entire country, looking for the perfect maiden, and when he found her, she claimed no interest in being his bride. He didn't know what to think. Perhaps she just didn't realize what a catch he was.

"Wait. Let me explain. I offer you the life of a Princess. You shall want for nothing. And, best of all, you will climb into bed with this every night." he said, moving his hands up and down in the air, indicating his torso. "I've determined that you are perfect. Do you not realize the honor which I pay you?"

The maiden thought about what he had said. Then she shook her head.

"Uh-uh. Being royalty is no excuse for acting rude, hurtful, and uncaring, all of which you have been in your search for a wife, crushing the feelings of many a hopeful maiden who didn't meet up to your standards."

She spun around so fast, splaying the lavender chiffon of her dress in a swirl around her ankles, revealing her matching lavender shoes. But she twisted her ankle, breaking off the heel of her left shoe.

"The man I marry should be kind and loving. He should care about the feelings of others. I can't marry a self-centered egomaniac like you!" she exclaimed over her shoulder as she hobbled away in her broken shoe.

Prince Geoffry bent, picking up the broken heel, as he started after her. "Wait! Don't you want your heel back?" he cried, holding out the abandoned heel. "What's your name?"

But alas, she hobbled around a curve in the road and was gone, without looking back.

"Stupid girl!" he yelled after her as he stood there with the broken piece of footwear in his hand.

He was tempted to run after her, but then it occurred to him that if she was stupid enough to run off without her heel, she couldn't possibly be perfect. For that matter, how could she be perfect if she didn't adore him? His bride could not have the slightest imperfection. Obviously, this maiden wasn't the one he sought, after all.

Discouraged, he threw the lavender heel as far as he could. He was a strong Prince, and the heel went flying into the deepest part of the forest where the undergrowth was so thick no man could not tread there without risking being tangled in it for eternity.

His footman, who was still a goat, bleated at him, drawing his attention away from the heel he'd thrown, which the maiden he had lost.

"If I want your opinion, I'll ask for it," he said to the goat. "There will be other maidens more perfect than the likes of her." And off they went down the path, in the opposite direction that the maiden had gone, once again in search of a maiden who was perfect.

Several weeks went by, and still, Prince Geoffry failed to find a maiden who was absolutely perfect. Although he met with many who were quite beautiful, none could match the beauty of the maiden who had broken the hag's curse on him. She had been kind, and lovely, and graceful, the most beautiful maiden he had ever seen. Try as he might, he couldn't seem to shake her image from his mind. As he lay atop his feather bed at night, he could think of nothing else, and if he managed to drift off into slumber, she was there in his dreams, surrounded by a golden aura.

Once, after a restless night, he arose to find that his goat of a footman had eaten his royal slippers. That was the last straw. Those shredded slippers just encapsulated all that had gone wrong in his life since meeting that old hag. He ranted as he paced around his royal bedchamber, grabbing his own hair and pulling, as if he were trying to rip it out of his head, his eyes bulging from their sockets.

"I'm the perfect Prince. How could she refuse me? Why do I want her when she's not perfect? I need her to want me, to love me. If she loved me, she'd be perfect."

Prince Geoffry picked up his glass of wine, but finding it bitter to the taste, he smashed it against the hearth, sending splinters of fine crystal flying in every direction. He ranted and paced and until he had worn himself to a frazzle.

Catching a glimpse of his reflection in his looking glass, he looked like he'd been through a tornado, and so did his bedchamber. His luscious chestnut hair stood on end in every direction; his clothes were ripped and tattered. The royal books and his other belongings were scattered about the floor amid purplish-red puddles and thousands of tiny shards of glass.

The goat took one look at him and ran away, bleating as if he'd seen a ghost. Prince Geoffry caught sight of the goat, who used to be his footman, just as he bolted for the door and smashed the decanter with the remaining wine on the lintel of the entrance portal in a less than fond farewell.

Prince Geoffry dropped to his knees, sobbing. His anger had run its course, but even though he still told himself she wasn't the right maiden for him, one sentence kept running through his head. "If she loved me, she'd be perfect."

Finally spent, he could not rest until he admitted to himself that he did indeed want the fair maiden with the lavender shoes to be his bride. Once he had done that, and determined to earn her love, he finally drifted off into a much needed, dreamless sleep.

The maiden, Lilly, was in great distress, as she had been ever since the day she'd met the goat and the frog who had turned out to be the Prince. She'd found the frog to be adorable, and even though he was quite handsome as the Prince, his reputation preceded him as being rude and even downright mean to all the maidens whom he hadn't found to be perfect.

Everyone knew that no one was perfect. Everyone except the stupid Prince, who thought himself to be perfect, yet was far from it. He was arrogant and rude, yet he just assumed any girl would desire to marry him. So why couldn't she get him out of her head?

"I just can't figure it out, Penelope," she said to her pig. "What I know about the Prince is not appealing, but I can't stop thinking about him. He is certainly handsome, not to mention how what a cute frog he made. Do you think it's possible that I might overlook his many flaws?"

Penelope snorted twice and gave out a squeal and ran in a circle.

"Oh, you are such a romantic, Penelope," Lilly said. "Why, even if I decided to take him up on his hasty proposal, with all the men guarding the castle, I'd never even get across the drawbridge."

The pig snorted four times, then spun in a circle, settling in for a little nap.

"Fine, just leave me to figure this all out on my own," Lilly said, looking down at her prize pig, who was turning out to be not much of a prize. There had to be someone who could find a solution.

Lilly paced while Penelope snored, thinking as hard as she could, until finally, she had an idea. "I know," she said aloud, holding a finger in the air as though it was a light bulb which had just gone on. "I'll go see Hilda, the hag who lived on the mountain. She will know what to do."

She packed up a basket of goodies with lots of sweets to soften up the old hag. Then she wrapped her violet velvet cloak around her and put the basket on her arm.

"Come on, you lazy pig," she said, tickling Penelope into wakefulness with her bare toe. Since she'd broken the heel on one of her lovely lavender shoes, she didn't have another pair. She slipped the leash over the pig's head, and they were off to visit the hag on the mountain.

When Prince Geoffry awoke from his long-needed slumber, he realized he now had another problem. Although he'd come to terms with the fact that he, the perfect Prince, was in love with an imperfect maiden, and although he had determined to win her heart, he had no idea where to find her.

The one thing that could have led him to her was the heel of her lavender shoe, and like an idiot, he had thrown it deep into the forest. Realizing what a foolish thing that had been to do, he wondered briefly if perhaps he'd been mistaken, and he himself was not perfect.

Then he returned to his senses and knew this couldn't be, exclaiming aloud, "Of course, I'm perfect. I'm the perfect Prince!"

He called and called for William, his footman goat, to no avail. So, he set out on a quest to find the heel to the maiden's lavender shoe on his own, traveling deep into the darkest, most overgrown part of the forest, where he thought he remembered throwing her heel.

The undergrowth was thick indeed, and branches and vines snagged his clothes and entwined his shiny black riding boots. But he was determined to win the heart of the stupid girl who had shunned him and make her into the perfect woman of his dreams, and so, he continued to search for years... and years... and years.... Until finally, he emerged, old and gray with the lavender heel in hand.

William, the goat, had run himself out trying to track down the Prince and was resting just outside the thicket. He gave out a loud bleat, rising slowly to his feet, as old goats will tend to do, when he saw Prince Geoffry emerge from the thicket.

The Prince was happy to see William, and crawled over to him, throwing a bony arm around his neck, but the extra weight sent them both tumbling to the ground. The goat was not strong enough to bear the weight.

"What's the matter with you, you old goat?" Prince Geoffry said as he regained his footing and rose to a standing position, straightening up to his full height. But when he got a good look at the goat, who was struggling to right himself once more, he realized that, indeed, was the problem. His former footman really was an old goat now.

He held up the lavender heel and gazed at it in wonder. Had he been searching for this silly heel for that long?

He ran over to the goat and grabbed the brass bell which hung around his neck, bending to gaze into it. What he saw staring back at him was an old, old man, with yellow teeth which sat crooked in his mouth, and long scraggly white hair which hung limply around his grimy, dirt-strewn face. When he looked down, he discovered that his ragged clothes were so shredded that there was barely any cloth to cover himself with.

He didn't recognize the man who stared back from his reflection. It couldn't be him. There was nothing perfect at all about that man, looking back from the shiny bronze surface. Nothing remained of the perfect black locks he remembered, or the perfectly white smile.

And as he watched, the man from his reflection began to cry, and his tears washed away streaks of dirt from his face, revealing just enough of the perfect skin, if a bit wrinkled, below the grim so that the Prince could no longer deny that the man in the goat's bell was indeed, his own reflection.

But how could this be? He scratched his head in confusion. He had always been the perfect Prince. But now, he had wasted so many years searching for the not-so-perfect maiden of his dreams, and he'd discovered he was no longer perfect. Now, even if he discovered the identity of the maiden which he sought, and if she did turn out to be perfect, she wouldn't want him. .

Prince Geoffry buried his face in the goat's fur and cried his eyes out at his own not-so-perfect fate.

He'd been a fool. Why hadn't he been kinder? He realized now that he had never truly been perfect, but instead had been blind to his own faults and overly sensitive to the faults of others.

After he cried himself out, he wiped his face with a ragged sleeve and helped the poor old goat back up onto his wobbly old legs. "

Why didn't you tell me I wasn't perfect?" he asked.

The goat gave a loud, rather rickety bleat and head butted him, knocking Prince Geoffry over, causing him to land rather hard on his bony old butt.

"Okay, so you did try to tell me," the Prince said, shaking his head as he picked himself up off the ground. He ran his hand over the goat's back, smoothing his wiry fur. "I'm sorry, old friend. I guess I deserve that. How could I have been so foolish?"

The goat gave out several loud bleats, backing away from the Prince, shaking his head rapidly. Prince Geoffry looked up to see a large pig soaring in on a pair of fluffy lavender wings and landed at his feet with a scroll of parchment in its mouth.

Prince Geoffry bent down and took the parchment from the pig's mouth and opened it up so he could read it.

It said:

Prince Geoffry,

If you still wish to find the lovely Lilly, come to Hilda's cabin on the mountain and make all your wishes come true.

"Who is Lilly?" Prince Geoffry asked.

The goat butted him lightly, making him drop the lavender heel. When he bent to pick it up, he had an epiphany.

"Is Lilly the name of the maiden whom I seek?" he asked aloud.

The goat bleated loudly.

Prince Geoffry scratched his head. "But..., who is Hilda, and how do I find her cabin on the mountain? It's a big mountain."

The parchment shook in his hand. As he looked down at it, new words appeared before his eyes.

Just follow the flying pig.

"Oh," he said, turning his attention to the pig. "I suppose the lavender wings should have told me you belonged to my love. By all means, lead on."

The pig began to flap his wings, but Prince Geoffry delayed the takeoff when he realized that the goat, who had once been his footman, wasn't following. "Wait," he commanded the pig. "I can't go without my old friend, William."

The goat bleated and butted him with his horns, lightly.

"I will not go without you," he said, looking into the goat's eyes. "I've wasted so many years selfishly, not appreciating you or your loyalty, but no longer. If you are too old to make the journey, then I will stay right here with you."

Just then, the pig came up, snorting. It turned around and backed up in front of the goat. It lowered itself to its knees, snorting loudly at the goat.

The goat bleated.

The pig snorted.

The goat stepped gently onto the pig's back, straddling the pig with a hoof on either side of each wing. Then, the pig snorted at the goat a few more times, flapped its wings and rose off the ground. The goat bleated loudly as they took to the air, and Prince Geoffry had to run to keep up.

The maiden, Lilly, was the first to spot the strange creature in the sky as it came in for a landing. She was at the well, fetching water for Hilda, the hag. As the beast approached, she could see that it had the lavender wings which the hag had enchanted Penelope with, but it was much bigger than Penelope and not really pig-shaped at all.

"Hilda, something is coming," she called out to the hag, squinting into the sun for a better view of the incoming beast. "Is this something that you cooked up?"

The hag came out of her cabin, letting her gaze follow that of Lilly. "That's not one of mine," she said. "I've never seen anything like that. What is it?"

But when the beast finally landed, it was just Penelope with the goat on her back. She landed with a thud and tumbled over onto her side, dumping the goat.

"I sent you to fetch the Prince, Penelope," Lilly said. "Instead, you brought me a goat?"

Penelope got to her feet, snorting and sniffing.

"I know that goat," said the hag. "That's the Prince's footman. He acted like a stuffy old goat, so I turned him into one. Ha!"

The goat bleated.

"But where is Prince Geoffry?" Lilly asked, disheartened. "I paid the hag a high price to get her to enchant you with wings, so you could find my true love. What happened?"

Penelope snorted three times, and then sat on her haunches. The goat sat down next to her and nuzzled his nose against her snout.

"Hello!" came a voice from across the meadow and all eyes turned in that direction.

A very old man came hobbling through the meadow towards them. The darn pig had messed everything up. Instead of her Prince, she now had a goat and a rickety old man. How could things get any worse? "Who is that?" Lilly asked.

Penelope squealed loudly, then stretched her front legs out straight in front of her and laid her head down on them in defeat.

The goat bleated a few times, then laid down next to her.

"Oh my," said the hag, "I do believe that is the Prince. Breaking my spell must have accelerated the aging process for him. Oh dear. That wasn't planned."

Tears escaped the corners of Lilly's eyes when she heard this. It was all too much. Once she figured out that she loved the Prince despite his many imperfections and flaws, she learned he was too old. "Just great," she said, stomping her foot in the dirt. "I've gone to all this trouble, and I still don't have the love of my life to wed."

"What do you mean?" said Hilda. "He's right there coming through the meadow. You said you loved him despite his flaws. So, being old is just one more flaw."

Lilly thought about this long and hard as she watched the old and not so perfect Prince approaching. She had traded her favorite pig to Hilda to have her prince found and brought here, but this was not the arrogant prince whom she remembered. Perhaps there had been other changes while he was away. Lilly decided she would just wait and see.

When Prince Geoffry finally hobbled through the front gate and up the path toward the cabin, he stopped short, looking over the party waiting to greet him. There was the maiden, Lilly, sitting on the edge of the well. Penelope the flying pig stood at her feet, and the goat who used to be his footman stood next to her, nuzzling her back between her wings...; and then he set eyes on Hilda.

"You...! You!" he exclaimed, pointing a bony finger at the hag. "Why did you send that pig to bring me here? Haven't you made me suffer enough with your stupid curse?"

"Oh, what are you crying about?" said Hilda. "That curse was removed long ago."

"Because of you, I lost everything," he cried.

"What did you lose?" Hilda said, aiming a sharp pointed fingernail at him. "You have an entire kingdom and are richer than most men can ever dream of being. You've lost nothing but the time you were a frog. So, what's the problem?"

"Kingdoms and riches! What are they worth?" he said. "What I lost is worth more than ten kingdoms and all the riches in the world."

"What? What did you lose that was worth so much?" Hilda said with a hint of sarcasm. "What would you trade for all the kingdoms and riches of the world?"

"Because of you and your stupid curse, I lost the best friend I ever had when you turned William into a goat," said Prince Geoffry.

The goat bleated loudly in agreement.

"Because of you, I lost the perfect wife, the love of my life," he continued, ignoring the interruption.

Lilly's ears perked up at that. Was he talking about her? Did he value her, after all?

"Now hold on," said Hilda. "The way I got it, your losing the girl had nothing to do with my curse. You messed that one up all on your own by being rude and inconsiderate, and full of yourself."

"It's all true," he said, a tear rolling down his cheek. "I was a fool, thinking of no one but myself. Please..., I've learned that I'm not perfect. Couldn't you help me get back those I have lost? I'll pay any amount you like. I'll pay for your hospitality from that day so long ago."

"Even if I wanted to help you, look at you now," Hilda said. "You're old and all used up. What makes you think she would want you?"

That old hag, thought Lilly. Hilda knew that Lilly wanted Geoffry despite his many faults. It was why she had come to Hilda for help in the first place.

The Prince hung his head in shame. "You're right, of course," he said. "But I'd still like the chance to apologize for my behavior and return the heel for her shoe, which I searched for all these years."

"Well then, tell her," said Hilda, pointing in Lilly's direction. "She's right there."

Prince Geoffry turned to look at Lilly, as if he'd been so focused on the hag that he hadn't really seen her there before. When his gaze fell upon her, she felt like an insect under a magnifying glass. Then he opened his eyes wide as recognition dawned on his face and he raised a bony finger to point at her. "You're the maiden, aren't you?"

Lilly nodded her head silently, suddenly feeling shy.

"Why, I didn't recognize you," he said, kneeling down in front of her and taking her hand in his. "I hope you will forgive me. I guess we've all changed over the years. Too bad we can't turn back the clock and take back all the time we've wasted."

When he raised her hand to his lips, brushing them across the back of it lightly, Lilly nearly swooned. This was not the same inconsiderate Prince who she had encountered that day so long ago. This Prince was gallant despite his age, and charming and considerate. She knew they were really one and the same, but she couldn't get over how much he had changed.

"Maybe there is a way," said Hilda. All heads turned her way.

The pig snorted.

The goat bleated.

Lilly and Prince Geoffry both looked at the hag with raised brows.

"I know of a spell," Hilda said. "It's been a while since I've used it, so I may have to look it up and refresh my memory, but I think it might work."

Prince Geoffry looked skeptical. "And why would you help me?" he asked. "Why did you bring me here in the first place?"

"Because I asked her to," said Lilly, rising from the edge of the well to look him in the eye. Then she turned her attention to Hilda. "But he's right, you know. Whatever you are thinking of doing, you already have my favorite pig. I have nothing else to bargain with."

"Oh, it's not that I can't pay her," said Prince Geoffry. "The hag was right when she said I still have my kingdom and its riches. But she also put a curse on me, turning me into a frog when last we met. I just can't help but wonder why the change of heart?"

"Look, I'll tell you why," said Hilda, scurrying around her garden, picking plants and herbs to concoct whatever spell she had in mind. "I cursed you because you were rude and had no respect for anyone but yourself. Now, it's obvious that you've changed, and I think it is only fair that you have a second chance. Besides, I promised Lilly I'd help her, and she's got it bad for you. Now just wait here while I gather a few more things from inside." With that, she turned and went back into the cabin, leaving Lilly alone with Prince Geoffry.

"Um...," Lilly said, shifting her weight from foot to foot as she tried to think of something to say. "I'm sorry that I rejected you without getting to know you first. I listened to what they said about you and didn't give you a fair chance."

"It's okay," he replied. "Most of what they said was true. I'm sorry I was searching for a maiden who didn't exist to be my wife. I've learned that I'm not perfect anyway, but I'm afraid that now, it is too late. We're both too old."

"Yeah, I guess we are," Lilly said as a heaviness fell over her heart. "I don't expect you'd want an old wife. I understand."

"What? No! I didn't think that you would want an old fart like me," he said. "You... why you are still as beautiful as ever."

Lilly felt herself blush. She couldn't have dreamed

Just then, the hag came out of the cabin carrying her big black cauldron. "Okay, kiddies. Hold tight," Hilda said, reaching into the cauldron and scooping up a handful of the powdery concoction inside.

Then she threw it at the couple with a big poof of smoke. When it cleared, they both were as young as they had been that day so long ago, when they'd shared their first kiss as maiden and frog.

Then the hag reached in the cauldron and pulled out another fistful of the powder, throwing it at the goat and the pig with another big poof. When the smoke cleared, William stood next to a beautiful maiden dressed in maid's attire.

Lilly threw her arms around Prince Geoffry, and he returned her embrace. Then she turned to Hilda. "This is wonderful, Hilda," she said. "I knew you were a softie."

William gazed into Penelope's eyes, and they held each other, smiling.

"Yes, it appears I have misjudged you," said Price Geoffry. "I apologize for my previous treatment. You are indeed a wonderful human being."

Hilda planted her fists on her hips and stomped her foot to get their attention. "Not one word from either of you. If either of you utter a word of this," she said, pointing a pointed fingernail at the Prince, "I swear I'll turn you into a toad this time. The irreversible kind." Then she turned and looked at Lilly. "And I'll turn you into a fly, so he can swallow you whole."

Lilly turned to look at her Prince, and their eyes met in an immediate understanding. They both turned to Hilda, raised their right hands and spoke in unison, "Never a word. We promise."

Kaye Lynne Booth

Kaye Lynne Booth lives, works, and plays in the mountains of Colorado. With a dual emphasis M.F.A. in Creative Writing and a M.A. in Publishing, writing is more than a passion. It's a way of life. She's a multi-genre author, who finds inspiration from the nature around her, and her love of the old west, and other odd and quirky things which might surprise you.

She has short stories featured in the following anthologies: *The Collapsar Directive* ("If You're Happy and You Know It"); *Relationship Add Vice* ("The Devil Made Her Do It"); *Nightmareland* ("The Haunting in Carol's Woods"); *Whispers of the Past* ("The Woman in the Water"); Spirits of the West ("Don't Eat the Pickled Eggs"); and *Where Spirits Linger* ("The People Upstairs"). Her paranormal mystery novella, *Hidden Secrets*, and her short story collection, *Last Call*, are both available in both digital and print editions at most of your favorite book distributors.

When not writing, she keeps up her author's blog, *Writing to be Read*, where she posts reflections on her own writing, author interviews and book reviews, along with writing tips and inspirational posts from fellow writers. In addition to creating her own imprint in *WordCrafter Press*, she offers quality author services, such as editing, social media & book promotion, and online writing courses through *WordCrafter Quality Writing & Author Services*. As well as serving as judge for the *Western Writers of America* and sitting on the editorial team for Western State Colorado University and *WordFire Press* for the *Gilded Glass* anthology and editing *Weird Tales: The Best of the Early Years 1926-27*, under Kevin J. Anderson and Jonathan Maberry.

In her spare time, she is bird watching or gardening, or just soaking up some of that Colorado sunshine.

The Nutcracker

By Roberta Eaton Cheadle

Sullen, angry, and dressed in a long sleeved and skirted black dress, Irene shuffled after her parents down the long flight of stairs. Her thick soled leather boots clumped noisily on the concrete and the backpack, containing her weighty journal, bounced unpleasantly against her lower back.

This stupid hard hat is giving me a headache. It's probably going to give me lice too, she thought resentfully.

There were people in front of her and people behind her, all wearing face masks in accordance with the regulations.

I hate people. Why did my parents force me to come? I also hate caves, the dark, and fossils. They should have brough Alex. He'd love this.

Her heart rate increased, pushing the blood faster around her body. It raced through her arteries and veins and drummed in her ears.

The tour stopped. The guide was showing them some boring fossil or other.

"... Little Foot ... nearly complete Australopithecus fossil skeleton ..."

I can't even hear what he's saying through that stupid mask.

The tunnel walls moved. Irene caught the movement in her peripheral vision. They moved again. Pushing closer to the line of people on the stairs.

"Get out," the wall whispered. "We don't want humans in our caves. You've destroyed enough. Get out!"

The tunnel wavered and spun. A wave of panicked nausea washed over her.

Is this real or is it a hallucination. Walls don't talk! Am I going crazy?

The taste of bile permeated her mouth. It was bitter. She swallowed hard.

I must act normally. Mom will have me back at that awful psychiatrist if I have a panic attack. He's already threatened to admit me if I don't improve on the medication.

Irene remembered the last visit to the doctor, who she privately called The Nutcracker. *He's there to crack nuts, like me.*

"How is your anxiety, Irene?" Dr Jamison asked her. "Are the tablets I prescribed helping you?"

"I don't feel better," she answered innocently. "I'm still afraid all the time and I can't concentrate or sleep at night."

Dr Jamison had written a new script increasing the dosage of the antidepressant to 60 milligrams a day. He also added a pill for acute anxiety.

"If the medication doesn't improve her anxiety and panic attacks, Mrs Harrison, we'll have to look at admitting her to hospital," he said, handing the script to her mother.

The medication makes me feel terrible. The more I take the more agitated I become. My reasons for living become obscure and anxiety threatens to overwhelm me. This is not the first-time walls have spoken to me. Why can't Mom see it's making me worse?

Unable to confide in her mother, Irene recorded her panic attacks and overwhelming sense of doom in her journal. It was her soul and she carried it with her all the time. Re-reading her written expressions of hopelessness, fatigue, and worry comforted her in some strange way.

A collection of articles about the effects of global warming and plastic pollution of the oceans and water systems were carefully tucked into a plastic sleeve at the back of the book. Irene never re-read them. They were reminders of her friendship with Sonia.

The stairs ended and the tour entered a dark, gloomy cave.

The tour guide pointed out a rock formation shaped like the head of an elephant.

The rocky formation was lined, creating an illusion of the thick wrinkled skin of a real elephant. Gazing at it, fascinated, Irene gasped when the fantasy mouth opened.

"How dare you look upon me, spawn of murderers. Your race is responsible for the near extermination of mine. Humanity will pay for its crimes. Just you wait!"

The rock rippled and cracked. A large, bloody hole formed in the creature's head; the edges ragged and dark with congealed tissue. Splodges of gore and white brain matter covered the wall around the elephant. Where once two shining ivory tusks had graced this magnificent animal, two serrated-edged holes clotted with old blood remained.

Why am I seeing this? What is going on? I'm going crazy, I really am!

Dropping her head, Irene gazed at the floor. The muscles in her arms and legs twitched and nausea rolled around her stomach.

Thoughts of Sonia filled her mind. Beautiful Sonia with her bright blue eyes and dark brown hair. Irene had met Sonia on the first day of school and they'd been friends ever since. Irene wanted to be just like Sonia. But now, Sonia was dead, her body rotting in a neglected graveyard.

"I feel so miserable and guilty when I read about the Holocene Extinction, Irene," Sonia had confided.

"Humanity is causing the sixth mass extinction on Earth through habitat destruction, deforestation, hunting, and pollution. We've filled the oceans with plastic debris and filled the air with carbon dioxide. It makes me so sad." Sonia's lovely eyes were clouded with pain.

"What right does humanity have to destroy the planet for all other living creatures. Even the pandemic, which is directly linked to human abuse of wild animals, has not made a difference. Businesses, in the name of economic growth, just carry on defiling, breaking, and destroying."

Looking at her intently, cheeks flushed with passion, Sonia burst out: "The worst part is that the destruction is sanctioned by governments. The very people we elect to protect our rights."

Oh Sonia, why did you leave me. I need you. Walls are speaking to me and turning into butchered animals.

Sonia had plunged into a depression from which she could see no way out. She'd resolved her pain six months previously by taking her own life.

The death of Sonia had horrified Irene's mother. Mrs Harrison had responded by sending her daughter to Dr Jamison.

Irene missed Sonia, her childhood friend. She could find little joy in life now, with Sonia gone and endless articles about the effects of climate change on the planet. When Sonia was alive, they would discuss them and look for ways they could contribute to saving the planet.

"Our generation still has time to turn things around," Sonia would declare optimistically. "We can make a difference even now by reducing our carbon footprint."

I don't know why Sonia lost hope for the future. She was always such a positive person. If she couldn't see anything to look forward to, how can I? She was so clever and knew so much.

Irene still preserved new articles in her journal. She read them once although their content increased her fractured sense of displacement and wretchedness. To not read and retain these reports would be a betrayal of their friendship.

Grief and loss whirled around her, making her throat constricted and her eyes pricky.

Wrap up your emotions, Irene ordered her mind. *Wind them up in a spider web, tighter and tighter.*

Shuffling after the group, anger at her parent's generation consumed her memories of Sonia.

Generation X, the generation that did nothing to stop global warming. The generation who destroyed the planet for my generation.

The group walked onto a platform. Switching on the lights, the guide illuminated the still, black waters of an underground lake.

"... no-one knows how deep the lake is ... the geology of the caves like a Swiss cheese, and where the pockets submerge, they fill with water...," said the guide.

Starring down into the dark lake, Irene sighed with pleasure at its mirror-like surface. It glittered and glimmered. Tiny ripples interrupted its smooth veneer. They picked up the dim light and transformed into lines of silver.

How wonderful. It looks just like Mom's antique mirror.

Mom's mirror stood on a carved wooden frame in the study. Its silvery face was marred by patches of black and tiny wrinkles. Irene enjoyed looking at herself in this mirror. It distorted her face slightly and, in places, her reflection disappeared into the dark stains.

It's like my heart and spirit – distorted and smudged with darkness.

"The guide is going to show us the minute creatures that live in the water." Her mother's voice seared through her absorbed pleasure in the shining water. "Why don't you come and have a look, Irene. It's interesting."

"No thanks, Meredith. I'd rather stay here and watch the water."

"Okay, suit yourself." Disappointment and hurt tinged her mother's tones.

Guilt momentarily clutched Irene's heart. Her recent use of her mother's first name had caused discord at home, but she clung to her decision to dissociate herself from her parents.

Hardening her heart, Irene turned her face away.

Wrap up your emotions. Tighter. Tighter.

Returning her focus to the water, she contemplated it.

How serene it is. So peaceful. It reminds me of The Nutcracker on Ice. I can almost see the dancers hiding just beneath that sparkling surface. They are dressed in beautiful white tutus, with white satin slippers on their feet.

... she could hear the music. Strains from Tchaikovsky's ballet tinkled in her ears. It was faint, but she recognised it immediately.

... she could see the dancers. Lustrous shapes moved just beyond her vision.

"Attention ladies and gentlemen, boys and girls, we're moving on now," the guide announced.

Irene peered back into the water. So harmonious ... so enticing.

Furtively, she slipped behind a jutting rock, out of sight of the tourists.

Moments later, the lights went out, plunging her into darkness.

The sound of footsteps faded away. Irene reached into her bag, fumbling around until she recognised the shape of her torch.

Switching it on, the water lit up immediately. Tantalising. The music started up again and the luminescent shapes resumed their dancing.

Now she could smell the popcorn and chocolate Dad always bought for her when they attended the ballet. A delightful mixture of oil, salt, and rich cocoa.

Beneath the rippling silver water, she could see the faces of the dancers. Their long hair was piled up into skillful buns, the type of hairstyle Irene had tried, but never managed to achieve. Their limbs were pale and gleaming.

Reaching out their arms towards her, they called: "Come and dance with us, Irene. It's lovely down here. So peaceful. Such lovely music. Come and dance." Their voices were soft and persuasive.

They must be real. Nothing this beautiful and graceful could be a hallucination.

Putting down her backpack, Irene climbed over the guardrail, torch clenched between her teeth.

The music played on ... sweet and full of happy memories.

The rocks were slippery as she stood on the edge of the lake, a sweet childlike smile on her face.

A long-fingered hand broke the surface of the water. It reached out and gripped Irene's right foot.

Irene shuddered, its flesh, cold and fishlike against her warm living skin.

Fear clenched her stomach and she tried to wrench her foot free. The fingers, tipped with black fingernails, held on tightly. The hand yanked hard.

Tumbling through the air, Irene fleetingly saw the lovely faces of the dancers transform. Sharp teeth dominated their white, dead faces.

Splash!

Black water filled Irene's eyes, ears, and mouth. She sank quickly, her cumbersome boots and drenched skirt pulling her down ... down.

Oh my God, they are real.

***

Meredith Harrison closed Irene's journal. Tears leaked from her swollen eyes and ran, unchecked, down her pale cheeks.

A large hand touched her shoulder, offering support.

"I'm so shocked, Bill, at what I've just read. I had no idea she was so disturbed and troubled. I thought the medication was helping her, but she was having hallucinations, dizzy spells, and nausea. Why didn't she tell me? Why didn't she let me help her?"

The hand squeezed gently. Meredith looked up into his tear-filled eyes.

"And all these stories about the effects of global warming and the destruction of the animal kingdom," a sob erupted from her constricted throat.

"Irene never spoke to me about any of this – why didn't she tell me? I've never dwelled on the long-term effects of climate change. Juggling work and a family were hard enough without taking on a problem that seemed so remote from my daily life."

"But you do try, Meredith," Bill's voice was soothing. "You're always sorting rubbish and trying to recycle plastic."

"Yes, I've always tried in a small way to make a difference and reduce our carbon footprint as a family, but I was never prepared to give up the big things like air travel, road trips, and red meat. I felt that I worked hard and deserved to have nice food and holidays.

"I didn't know it concerned her so much. I could have done more. Would have if she'd discussed it with me. Why didn't she speak to me? Am I such a bad mother?"

"It's not your fault, Meredith. You must stop blaming yourself for Irene's death. You were a good mother and did you best to help her. You took her to a psychiatrist and followed his advice," Bill stoked her cheek, wiping away the tears. "It's not your fault. You're not a mental health expert and you did the best you could."

Bill handed her a leaflet. It was lightweight and folded many times from being inserted into a small box.

"This is the leaflet for Irene's anti-depressant. I think you should read it."

Meredith took the offered paper. Bill had circled a section in heavy black pen.

This medication may increase serotonin and rarely can cause
a serious condition called serotonin syndrome/toxicity ...

Speak to your doctor immediately if you develop any of the following symptoms: fast heartbeat, hallucinations, loss of coordination, severe dizziness, severe nausea/vomiting/ diarrhoea, twitching muscles, unexplained fever, unusual agitation/restlessness ...

Meredith seemed to crumple, assuming an appearance of great age and fragility.

"It's not your fault, Meredith," he repeated. "I don't think the medication was right for her and there is no way we could have known that."

Hunched over and small, she didn't react.

"You've got to pull yourself together. Think of Alex. He's lost his sister and only sibling. He needs you to be strong."

Uncurling in slow motion, Meredith straightened her shoulders and lifted her chin.

"It's going to change going forward, Bill. Never again will I placidly accept the advice of a doctor without doing my own research. And I'm going to warn other people who are suffering with depression not to ignore red flags. I'm going to start a blog and share our experiences. At least that's something positive I can do.

"As for climate change, I'm going to research what we can do to change our lifestyle and make a real difference. It is the least I can do for my daughter, for my Irene ... and for Alex too. We must do our bit to secure his future."

"Those are good ideas, Meredith, and I'll support you as much as I can."

Bill leaned over and kissed the top of her head. "Now come to bed and try to sleep. We can discuss your new projects again in the morning."

He took her hand and Meredith allowed him to lead her out of the room.

Glancing back as he turned out the light, she saw a flicker in her antique mirror. A vague impression of her daughter materialised. She was smiling. Or was it a grimace.

Meredith took a step back into the room, mesmerised by the face in the mirror.

Crack!

The glass broke in two. It split open like a ripe tomato, and dark water gushed wetly onto the carpet.

Help me, mother. Help me. Irene's shrieks echoed in her head.

Meredith clutched her chest, collapsing to her knees and then forward. Her head smacked the red and black patterned carpet with a thud. Blackness enveloped her.

Roberta Eaton Cheadle

Roberta Eaton Cheadle is a South African writer and poet specialising in historical, paranormal, and horror novels and short stories. She is an avid reader in these genres and her writing has been influenced by famous authors including Bram Stoker, Edgar Allan Poe, Amor Towles, Stephen Crane, Enrich Maria Remarque, George Orwell, Stephen King, and Colleen McCullough.

Roberta has short stories and poems in several anthologies and has two published novels:

* Through the Nethergate, a historical supernatural fantasy; and

* A Ghost and His Gold, a historical paranormal novel set in South Africa.

Roberta has ten children's books published under the name Robbie Cheadle.

Roberta was educated at the University of South Africa where she achieved a Bachelor of Accounting Science in 1996 and a Honours

Bachelor of Accounting Science in 1997. She was admitted as a member of The South African Institute of Chartered Accountants in 2000.

Roberta has worked in corporate finance from 2001 until the present date and has written seven publications relating to investing in Africa. She has won several awards over her 20-year career in the category of Transactional Support Services.

The Elevator Ritual

By Shelly Jasperson

I wasn't an idiot. I knew Lisa Henry had probably voluntarily climbed over the peeling white metal fence and flung herself into the shallow pool of algae-infested water. I just wasn't sure she was the one controlling her own body.

I'd spent hours poring over her blog entries and case files, pathetically obsessing over the incident while sitting in my parents' basement. My long, dark hair went days without a wash and my converses crossed under my legs for hours at a time, forming a sort of rigor.

Lisa's body had been found a week after she went missing, floating face down, already bloated. Her disappearance and the strange circumstances of her death created a media frenzy, before ultimately being deemed a suicide. But she had plans for the future and no history of mental illness. Why would she climb over the fence and jump into a shallow, unused pool? Was there a worse way to die than by drowning?

My breath seized just thinking about it.

Her tragedy had taken over my life. I couldn't move on until I did something about it. So, I said good-bye to my parents, who seemed happy to have their 26-year-old daughter out of the basement, and drove to the Chambray Hotel in southern California, the location of Lisa Henry's disappearance and death.

After five hours I finally stood in the lobby of the Chambray Hotel. Off-white walls towered high over my head and simple, dark furniture created classy vignettes in every corner, visited by limestone statues. A grand staircase with white marble steps grew out of the floor to the right of the hotel desk. Pillars stood guard over shiny, decorative alabaster flooring and swanky light fixtures. The entire area had an eerie golden glow.

I was here. Where she'd died.

My shoes slapped against the reflective flooring as I approached the front desk. A tidy, short man in his thirties with a dark goatee stood behind the desk and smiled at me. His nametag read, "Josh".

He gave me a patronizing grin that said he knew exactly why I was there. Did anyone come to the hotel without a morbid curiosity about the ghosts and infamous things that had happened here?

Except my curiosity was overwhelmed by my need to help her. The girl who was found in the shallow pool.

"Welcome to the Chambray. Do you have a reservation?"

I nodded and flipped through my black backpack. My sister used to handle reservations, commitments, and dates when we traveled together. My brain wasn't organized like that. But I'd never travel with Avery again and I knew I had to learn how to take care of myself.

"It's under the name, 'Alice Newton.'" I pulled out my wallet.

After Josh had given me my key, I nearly ran into a woman with wild, black hair wearing an off-white tracksuit and flip flops. Her face was creased with deep lines and her teeth were jagged and yellow. I hadn't known anyone else was even in the lobby.

"Excuse me! Sorry!" I backed away as my head mixed revulsion with guilt. She was just a nice old lady, not a ghost or murderer.

"Not a problem, dear." She reached out and grabbed my arm with a surprisingly tight grip. Her fingers were ice cold. She leaned in, breathing next to my ear with gasps and hitches. "Just be careful, dear. This place has quite a history, you know." She let go.

I gulped and pulled back. Yes, I knew the history. That was why I'd come. But I just nodded and said, "Thank you."

I backed away from her, hitting the metal leg of a black chair with my ankle and nearly falling into the slick leather. I shook my head. I shouldn't get distracted. I was here for a purpose.

I walked to the hotel elevators.

I watched my own face pale in the gold, reflective doors.

I couldn't stop my heart from hammering.

These elevators were the real reason I was here. They terrified me, but the most important thing I'd do would be inside them.

I closed my eyes and grimaced. Not now.

I dashed through the lobby, up the grand staircase that took me to the second floor. I could feel Josh's eyes on me from the desk. Judging and smirking. The old lady was gone. I took the stairway up until I reached the 7th floor.

By then, my breath was coming short and fast and my feet were languid and slow. The hallway had a musty smell, like old milk had been spilled and not cleaned up. The walls were brown, and the door frames were coated in white paint, covering nicks and dents. I opened my door and walked in.

The room was small with heavy coats of brown paint. A twin bed sat in one corner and an old porcelain sink sat in the other. A tiny bathroom was attached, with the light already on. I gulped.

So many terrifying things had happened at this hotel. Not the least of which were the ghost sightings. Hundreds of people had died here. And the last thing I wanted to do was see one of them. I dropped my backpack, tore the comforter off the bed, and draped it over the cracked mirror.

Sitting on the bed, I took a deep breath. I was already a bundle of nerves. How could I go to the elevator in the middle of the night and do the ritual in this state? I needed to calm down, meditate.

I still had a few hours before midnight.

I pulled off my shoes and sat back down on the bed. The mattress coils were faintly visible through the sheet and mattress protector. When I brought my legs up to sit cross-legged, the surface crackled like a sheet of paper.

I closed my eyes, rested my arms on my knees, and took a deep breath.

Avery stood behind my eyelids. She was at the barre in a light pink leotard and beige ballet shoes. She gracefully raised her arm before her and brought it out before ducking into a *demi plie*. Her dark hair cascaded down her back, silky as calm water. Then she left first position and moved her leg out, into second. Just basic warmups that appeared simple but were impossible for any normal person to do. Like me.

We'd started ballet at the same time. She'd taken to it like a gazelle leaping in a savanna, whereas I'd been awkward and floppy, graceless as a drunk giraffe.

I lay onto the bed, the springs jabbing into my back. After all the driving, I was exhausted and barely even cared. Within moments, I'd fallen fast asleep.

What felt like a second later, my nose itched with the feeling of thin strands sweeping across my skin. With my mind groggy and my eyes still closed, I pictured Lisa Henry sitting on the edge of my bed, leaning over my head, staring at my sleeping body.

Her face was expressionless and pale. But beyond the dark circles, her eyes plead, *Help me.*

That's why I was here. I was going to help her.

Lisa leaned lower, right over my face, and her hair slid through the crevices in my face, a few snaky tendrils prying between my eyelids, more in my nostrils, and thousands down my throat. The tresses multiplied and forced their way in, no matter how hard I shut my eyes and mouth. I couldn't move. My mind churned like a violent sea. Hair scratched my corneas, plugged up my nose, and filled my mouth. I gagged on the spiderweb-thin strands. I choked and thrashed internally, but I still couldn't move to save myself. She was suffocating me.

Suddenly, I sat up and opened my eyes, gasping for air and swiping at the orifices on my face.

No hair smothered me. I was alone in the room. I ran to the mirror and tore off the comforter. I only saw the scratches I'd just made with my own fingernails. Short, puffy red lines zigzagged from my lips to my chin and under my eyes to my cheeks.

I shuddered and leaned over, taking breaths between gasps and gags. Spittle dripped to the brown carpet in little pools.

It had been a dream. Every wound had been self-inflicted.

When I stood up, the clock read 11:50 pm.

I had to calm down. It was time.

I straightened my clothes, wedged my feet into my shoes, grabbed the instructions from my backpack, and opened the door to a dark, lonely hallway. I left my phone. A black window at the end of the hall beckoned me forward. A vague, ghostlike image of myself reflected back. Each step brought me closer to the elevator.

I glanced at the paper in my hand.

What if I'd written the directions down wrong?

No. I'd triple checked. They were correct. Shaking my head, I stopped before the elevators.

A pale woman, tinted an aged yellow, stared back at me in the mirrors on the doors. She looked terrified. I rubbed my eyes, as if that would change my expression. When that didn't work, I took a deep breath and pressed the button, anyway.

Lights above my head indicated that the elevator was slowly making its way to the seventh floor from the lobby.

Panic lit my insides like firecrackers. What if I was supposed to walk down to the lobby and get onto the elevator from there? What if I'd just ruined the whole ritual?

But when the elevator door opened, I closed my eyes and stepped in calmly, as if tiny explosions weren't going off in my head.

Mirrors lined the walls inside. The same scared woman followed me in. Dark hair framed her gaunt face. I steeled my resolve.

It was too late for Avery. But if it was possible to help Lisa, I had to try.

I pressed the lobby button, leaving a fingerprint. I didn't know where to look. My frightened face followed me from every direction. So, I found my shoes and focused on the scuff marks across the white toes. The elevator doors slid closed. I was trapped.

When the elevator grunted into action, I gasped and braced myself against the mirrored wall, touching fingertips with my doppelganger.

The elevator rattled and shook. Mechanic whirring lowered me to the lobby, where the door slid open.

The lobby was dimly lit. Nightlights next to the black chairs gave the space a golden glow. I had to step out of the elevator to truly start the ritual, but my body was frozen.

What were the chances it would actually work? How could choosing a series of floors transport me to another dimension? How crazy did I sound? But I'd been led here. When I'd read the instructions, something in me knew it was true. And whenever I'd watched a youtuber try it, I'd known it wouldn't work for them. You had to do it alone and they'd brought a camera. The instructions were precise.

Every step had felt correct, like I had some innate knowledge, like I was meant to do the ritual. Every choice had felt like the right choice.

I couldn't save Avery. She'd left her boyfriend's house that horrible night and disappeared into the mountains. Two days later, her body had been found face down in the water five miles away from her car. Why had she driven up the mountain? Why had she left her car and set off on foot for five miles in the dark? I gritted my teeth and clenched my jaw, more angry than sad. I couldn't save her. She was gone before I had the opportunity to try.

With Lisa, there was a video of her that the police had sent out. She stood in the elevator at this very hotel, pressing buttons and acting strange, unnatural. To me it was obvious. She'd performed the elevator ritual, gone into another dimension, and her body had come out possessed. That had to mean that her spirit was trapped in the other dimension somehow.

All she needed was a body.

I had one of those. And I wasn't doing much with it.

I stepped out, the spell broken. The doors closed behind me.

I glanced at the concierge desk, where Josh had relished in my discomfort. No one stood there now. And no creepy old lady stood close by to give me advice. I was all alone in the lobby of an eight-hundred room hotel. I took a deep breath. This was it.

I turned around and pressed the button before I could change my mind.

The elevator to the farthest right opened its doors.

I had no idea which elevator Lisa had taken. I hoped it didn't matter. I walked to the far-right elevator and stepped in.

Like the other elevator, mirrors bombarded me with my own image on every side, not tinted gold like the doors, but solid and clear.

I pressed the fourth-floor button and closed my eyes, swallowing a lump of fear.

Nothing happened. I might as well have done nothing. I waited for almost a minute. Was this some mechanical problem or was a ghost messing with me? I didn't have time for a ghost encounter. I pressed the button again, harder this time.

With a mechanical grinding, the elevator lurched upwards. I fell against the wall in surprise. The lights flickered in an electrical fit. This had to be normal. The building was over a hundred years old. Eventually, the lights decided to stay on and above my head, each floor indicator lit up one by one until the doors opened on the fourth floor.

The floor had cheap brown carpet and thick brown paint on the walls, much like the seventh floor. The baseboards and door frames were a stark white, marked with occasional black streaks and scrapes. The only identifying feature that let me know I wasn't on the seventh floor was the large plaque on the wall that read "Floor 4" in large, red letters.

The elevator doors closed before I remembered to touch a button. I pressed two and waited again as the elevator moved.

My legs wobbled involuntarily as I watched the door open and close on floor two. I pressed 6 and waited. After the fourth floor, my heart rate sped up. The lights flickered, as if in response. When I passed the fifth, I swallowed bile that had risen in my throat.

In about a minute, I'd have to press the 5th floor button and watch the woman get on.

According to the instructions for the ritual, a woman from the other dimension was supposed to enter the elevator when you reached the fifth floor. You weren't supposed to talk to her or even look at her. And if you did, horrible things would happen to you.

The fact that the consequences were so vague told me one of two things: either it was a story and the author got lazy or no one had ever survived an encounter with her. I'd researched the elevator ritual enough to know it wasn't just a story. So that only left that she'd never let anyone who saw her live.

After floor 6, I went back down to floor two. I pressed 10, which was the last floor I was supposed to go to before stopping on 5th and picking up the woman. Suddenly, I wished there were forty more steps before going to the fifth floor. Maybe I should just go back down to the lobby and start again? Maybe I'd messed something up?

The old elevator creaked and groaned up to the tenth floor, sputtering to a stop before opening up.

Everything had been going according to plan. No one had entered to interrupt my journey. But the thought of the woman terrified me so much I almost wished someone would wake up from their room on the tenth floor with a sudden need to use the elevator.

I searched the hallway. Brown walls. White trim. Red sign. I might as well have been the only person on earth. A part of me wanted to run out of the elevator and pound on the first door I saw so that I wouldn't be alone.

But the elevator doors closed, and my resolve faltered.

I had to do what I came here to do. I took a deep breath and pressed 5.

Sometimes the woman didn't even get on the elevator. Maybe I would get lucky.

They said the woman sometimes takes the form of someone you know. And she talks to you, tries to get your attention by any means. Coughing, begging for help, keeling over. Could I deny aid to someone who looked like my sister? Or who looked like Lisa, the girl I was trying to save?

It was best not to even look at her. Then I wouldn't know who she looked like.

The elevator stopped on the fifth floor. I turned around, faced the mirrored walls, and closed my eyes.

And waited.

The doors opened behind me.

My heart was beating through my chest.

A shuffling noise. Was it footsteps? Was she in the elevator with me? I froze and almost stopped breathing.

The doors closed. I was stuck in here with her.

Then I realized the major flaw in my plan. From here, I had to press the button for the first floor. If it took me to the tenth instead, I'd be free to roam the other dimension and look for Lisa.

How could I press the button if my eyes were closed, and the woman was between me and the buttons?

I slowly opened my eyes and looked down at my shoes. Black scuffs against off-white toes. I swallowed and let my eyes drift across the floor until they reached another pair of shoes. Her shoes.

My breath caught and I couldn't help shaking. She was right there. Not even a foot away.

But her shoes looked so ordinary. Solid black flip flops.

I don't know why, but I was almost expecting something from the 19th century with faded lace and buttons down the back. This woman could have been anyone. Would I have been scared of her if I'd passed her down the hall? What if this wasn't *the* woman, but the woman I'd met in the lobby? Or some random woman who was staying on the fifth floor? I probably seemed like an idiot. Maybe if I saw more of her . . .

I closed my eyes again and took a deep breath. She was supposed to look normal, familiar, even. That was how she caught you.

I maneuvered around the open toes, the pale calves, to the panel. Then I lifted my eyes.

"I'm not her."

I froze. Her voice sounded so normal. Not faint, like a ghost, or scratchy, like someone sick. It was clear and youthful and almost mocking. Like I should feel ridiculous for not looking at her. I couldn't fall for that. I didn't know exactly what she could do to me, but I needed to live.

I pressed the "floor 1" button and closed my eyes.

"I said," she raised her voice. "I'm not that woman. I know what hotel this is. I'm not her."

She shuffled behind me, agitated.

The elevator shifted and cranked into motion. Was it going down or up? If it was going down, I'd failed. But I couldn't open my eyes again. I couldn't chance it. Whatever happened, I'd just have to get off and hope I'd made it to the tenth floor. Don't think about her. Just pretend she isn't there.

I could sense movement behind me. I gulped down my fear and stayed still. She couldn't hurt me if I didn't acknowledge her. That was the rule, right?

A warm breeze blew my hair away from the back of my neck. But there was no breeze. It was her, blowing on my skin.

Goosebumps raised the hair on my neck. I shook. My chest constricted, as if my heart was beating as fast as it could against a tiny cage, not getting nearly enough air.

Had the elevator slowed down? Were we still moving?

A finger slid between strands of my hair. I felt warmth, a body coming closer. A mouth against my ear. I could feel her smiling.

She coughed, a wheeze with a slight whistle to it, and droplets of phlegm landed inside and around my ear.

A deep shudder started at my head and shot through my body, to my toes. I couldn't do this anymore. I pressed myself against the mirrored metal door and braced myself, gritting my teeth.

Every floor must have taken ten minutes to reach. The cranking ticked like the second hands of a clock. I'd never make it.

She wheezed and coughed again, until it turned into a hack. "You said you were going to help me!" She gagged and spluttered.

Lisa? Was the girl Lisa Henry? She'd been wearing flip flops when she'd been found. What if the rumors were wrong? What if she really needed help?

Tick, tick, tick.

She collapsed behind me, her body thudding onto the ground and convulsing. I pinched my eyes closed. Everything I'd read said not to engage. The evil woman was clever. Her coughs slowed and stopped.

I couldn't look. Guilt pounded a migraine into my head.

The doors slid open. In my periphery, I saw brown carpet just outside the elevator.

The lobby had hard floors, right? Only the upper floors were carpeted. Was it the tenth floor? The doors began sliding shut.

No. I couldn't be enclosed in the elevator with this girl again. I wouldn't. I made for the door.

With one swift motion, the girl struck her hand out for my foot.

I screamed and jolted away from her, landing on the carpet. I was outside the elevator. Somehow, I'd made it.

Taking deep breaths, I turned to watch the doors close behind me. But the moment before they did, I saw her face.

Inches off the floor, glaring at me with wide black holes for eyes and gray, lacerated cheeks. Her arm was still extended towards me, and she glared with intense hatred. She wasn't Lisa Henry. She was evil.

With the door closed, my mouth gaped and panic split through me like an ax. I'd looked at her. I'd seen her face. I shook uncontrollably as I took small steps backward.

I was so close. I was practically out! But I'd seen her.

The indicator at the top of the elevator lit floor 9, then floor 8. She was moving it.

Those black holes and that gray face hid behind my vision and came, unbidden, when I closed my eyes. She might not ever go away. But something else struck me.

I was on the tenth floor. I'd pressed one, but the elevator had brought me to the tenth.

It had worked.

I was in another dimension.

Had this happened to Lisa Henry? Is that why she died? Had she seen the woman on the elevator? Was that why she got stuck?

I shook my head. I had to believe I could still live. I'd done everything right. I'd completely ignored her. Maybe seeing her didn't count if you were already off the elevator. I had to believe that was right. I took a few steps, still seeing her face, inches off the floor, with dead, peeling skin surrounded by thick, dark hair.

I swallowed and steeled myself. I had to act, or it was all for naught.

Brown carpet. Brown walls. Thick white trim. Smudges on the baseboards. Smears of dirt on the walls. It looked just like the hotel in my dimension. What if I hadn't entered anywhere but the tenth floor? The elevator had been acting strange, maybe it was just an electrical failure that brought me up here?

There was only one way to tell.

"Lisa! Where are you?" I yelled, walking down the hall. How would she appear to me? As a spirit?

Then I saw her before me, her thin outline against a dark sky. Long, dark hair, terrified expression, and skinny, bare legs. She seemed to be floating just a few feet away. I couldn't see her feet.

I took a step towards her, my heart pounding, and she took a step towards me.

"Lisa?"

With a shaking hand, I reached out and touched a window.

It was me. My reflection.

I blew out a deep breath and shook my head.

None of this was real.

What was I doing here? Searching for the spirit of a girl I didn't even know, just because she reminded me of Avery? I blinked rapidly and then massaged my head, feeling a weight lift from me. For the last few months, I'd burrowed myself into a depressive hole, obsessing and willing to believe anything if it would help me get Avery back.

But the truth was nothing could get Avery back. And even if Lisa were really trapped somewhere in a dilapidated dimension and I gave her my body, that still wouldn't bring me any closer to my sister. It wouldn't help Avery at all.

I hadn't been sleeping well. I'd probably hallucinated the woman in the elevator.

I dropped my paper and sighed. I needed some sleep. For the first time in months, I was sure I would actually get some.

I turned to go down the stairs.

Every step brought me closer to my room, a quiet space. I could sleep all day and all tomorrow night if I wanted. My body might require that of me.

I reached my room and entered, chuckling. How had I convinced myself any of it was real? Even through my embarrassment, relief permeated through my whole being. Had I seriously been ready to throw my life away? I'd never find a career, fall in love, get married, have kids. How could I find so little value in all of that?

When I fell onto my bed and closed my eyes, the woman's dead, almost skeletal face popped up behind my eyelids again. I opened my eyes and took a deep breath. Over time, I could get rid of her.

I walked to the sink and splashed cold water on my face. Streaks of red scrawled across my cheeks.

The woman stood behind me.

I spun around.

She was still there. My body froze, a mannequin. My lungs clenched tight. I gaped.

I hadn't escaped her. She was as real as I was. As real as the scuffs on my shoes. As real as the scrapes on my face.

Her lip lifted in a snarl. "You abandoned me."

My brows furrowed and I gulped down a lump of fear. I shook my head.

I inspected her hair, slick and long, and her thin body in a familiar blue t-shirt from summer camp. It was Avery. My sister.

"Where have you been?" I gasped.

The holes where her eyes should have been, were as black as a cave. She scowled. "I've been here the whole time."

"How is that possible?" My sister had been in this hotel? I flipped through the images of her disappearance in my mind. Her faded red car parked in the forest, her boyfriend's distraught face, my parents' closed door.

I took a step back, shaking, until I hit the sink with my back. This couldn't be real. Avery wouldn't be this mad at me. Avery would never hate me this much. She hadn't just been my sister. She'd been my best friend. It couldn't be her. I combed my hands through my hair, pulling out strands, until I dipped onto the floor. My knees shielded me from the fake Avery.

If she wasn't Avery, how was she wearing the camp shirt? I looked down at her feet.

Scuffed up Converses. Where had the flip flops gone? I looked back up at her face.

Scratches tore deep gashes across her cheeks. Every wound had been self-inflicted.

It was my face.

She was me.

Once she could tell I'd put it together, she grinned, her mouth wide and teeth yellowed. I pulled at my own mouth, the teeth I'd neglected when I'd obsessed over someone else.

How was she me? I stared at her eerily familiar face as she walked towards the door and left the hotel room. Her hand gripped the doorknob and turned it. She wasn't a ghost, a spirit. I followed her into the dimly lit hallway.

"Where are you going?" I managed to squeak out.

She turned to me and smiled before continuing onward, stopping only once she arrived at the elevators. My mind swam. This had to be a dream. Who was this being inhabiting my body?

She leaned forward and pried her fingers between the doors of the elevator, using strength I never possessed. I looked cautiously at the button she hadn't pressed. The doors slid open.

The elevator wasn't there. There was black space interrupted by vertical metal cables.

She stepped forward, into the darkness.

Shelly Jasperson

Shelly Jasperson lives with her supportive husband, three active boys, a goofy corgi, and a fluffy booplesnoot. We don't speak of the birds. Her bachelors in Archaeology is hardly relevant, but she likes bringing it up, anyway. She's been writing for most of her life and has had several short stories published.

The Tinker's Gift

By Valerie B. Williams

Corporal Clarence Hutchinson remembered well the day Bartley Penfold arrived at Abrams House with a clatter and a song. His canvas-sided wagon bore the words "Penfold's Knife Sharpening & Other Repairs." Hidden metal objects clanged against each other in rhythm with the plodding steps of the large black dray horse. Penfold sang a hymn in a strong tenor voice as the wagon approached the wide front porch. He doffed his bowler hat at Mrs. Forsythe as he sang the final refrain, "bringing in the sheaves."

"Good afternoon, Madam." His gaze ran across the line of wounded soldiers in gray—sitting, standing, and leaning in front of the large house. "May I offer my services? I can sharpen surgical instruments, repair pots and pans, or work metal into any tool you need."

Penfold looked directly at Hutchinson and smiled, showing crooked yellow teeth. Trapped in the gaze of the tinker, Hutchinson felt light-headed. He looked away and immediately felt better. He stared hard at the blanket covering his lap, and what remained of his right leg, and listened as the man continued.

"I also happen to be an ordained minister. I could provide spiritual comfort to these brave men."

Mrs. Forsythe frowned and tapped her forefinger against closed lips before speaking. "All strangers are welcome to a meal and a night of rest at my home. If you can provide the services which you state, you may be able to stay longer."

"I will remain as long as I am helpful. I want nothing more than to support our soldiers in any way I can. Sadly, I am too old to don the uniform."

And as simply as that, Penfold was in.

Mrs. Forsythe was the mistress of Abrams House, a stately Virginia mansion which had been converted to a convalescent hospital. Her husband led a regiment currently fighting in Pennsylvania while she supported the cause at home. She was quite discerning, so her easy acceptance of Penfold had surprised Hutchinson. The man seemed a bit "off," but Hutchinson was the only one who noticed.

Penfold wasted no time getting to know everyone in and around Abrams House, from soldiers to slaves. His age showed in his deeply lined face and iron gray hair, but he was as spry as a spring lamb, moving easily around his forge as he repaired and constructed tools and instruments. As meticulous about his appearance as his work, he was never seen without a vest and cravat, hair oiled and slicked back. A small camp mirror dangled from his belt, assuredly for him to check that no hair was out of place.

After a few days working his trade for the hospital and for Mrs. Forsythe, he began making regular visits to the men in the ward, inquiring if they had any belongings in need of repair, and offering to pray with them if they wished. Most of the soldiers had few if any possessions, so Penfold could often be seen standing with head bowed, murmuring words intended only for the occupant of the cot.

Hutchinson declined all Penfold's offers of prayer, begging off as tired and in need of rest. The part-time preacher took the refusal in stride, with a yellow smile and a "God bless you, soldier," as he moved on to the next man.

Hutchinson woke from a midday doze to hear Penfold speaking to Private Evans in the adjoining cot. Evans had been feverish and coughing, spending much of his time wheezing in opium-induced sleep. The smell of mustard plasters rose from his overheated body.

"Would you like to see them?" asked Penfold.

"More than anything, sir. My little Charity will be three years old next month. She was hardly walking when last I saw her."

Hutchinson kept his back turned and feigned sleep. He heard a rustling of clothing, followed by a click.

"Oh!" gasped Evans. "Look! It's Eva. And there's sweet Charity. Hello! Hello!"

"They cannot hear you. Or see you. The mirror only allows you to view them, not speak to them."

Evans began to sob. "They look so happy."

"They are, except that they miss you. But they are proud of you. And the Lord will care for them after you are gone."

"Gone? But I'm going to return to them. As soon as I get better!"

"Of course, you will all be reunited. In God's time."

Hutchinson heard the stool creak as Penfold stood.

"Get some rest, my son."

The next morning Evans was a new man. Hutchinson awoke to find him perched on the edge of his cot, cheeks ruddy with life. The man even took a brief, although slow, walk around the ward. When Hutchinson touched Evans' shoulder, the heat that had radiated from his body was gone.

"Fever broke. That's what the doctor said. I feel well enough to walk out of here and home to my family."

"I don't think you're ready for that quite yet," said Hutchinson. "But you do look much better." He cleared his throat, then blurted out the question that had been foremost in his mind. "What did you see in Mr. Penfold's mirror?"

Evans' eyes widened and he smiled broadly. "My girls, moving about. Eva was hanging wash on the line while Charity played at her feet. It was like looking into the garden through a windowpane. Magical! You should ask him. I'm sure he'd let you see your family as well."

Hutchinson was not the only person Evans told. By the end of the day, the story of the tinker's magical mirror had spread throughout the ward. But Penfold was nowhere to be found. His wagon and forge still stood where they had for the past few weeks, but the man himself had disappeared.

The next day, Evans was discovered dead in his cot, all signs of his miraculous recovery gone. The body was ashen and shrunken, skin stretched tight as if all its moisture had fled. But the soldier had died with a smile on his face.

Penfold reappeared around mid-morning. He looked refreshed, as if he'd just woken from a long nap. He claimed to have taken a walk in the forest and gotten lost, returning to his wagon in the wee hours. He immediately offered to perform the burial service for the unfortunate Evans. Hutchinson's wheelchair couldn't negotiate the rocky path to the growing cemetery behind the stables, so he heard second-hand about the powerful sermon that brought Mrs. Forsythe to tears.

With Penfold's return, many soldiers began to beg for a glimpse into his mirror. He denied all requests except those of the sickest. Over the course of the next two weeks, three more soldiers had miraculous one-day recoveries, followed by an overnight death. All died smiling.

Rumblings of suspicion began. Soldiers stopped asking to look into Penfold's mirror, terrified that the vision would cost them their lives.

Mrs. Forsythe called Penfold to the library. Raised voices were heard, but eventually the door opened and the two walked out arm in arm. They went directly to the ward, where a slave banged on a bucket until the murmuring ceased and all attention turned to Mrs. Forsythe. Bartley Penfold stood next to her, head down and hands clasped. Hutchinson detected a smirk on the tinker's face—a face noticeably smoother than when he arrived at Abrams House.

"Gentlemen," said Mrs. Forsythe. "It has come to my attention that you believe Mr. Penfold here," she nodded toward him, "is responsible for the deaths of Evans, Sullivan, Murgatroyd, and Fitzpatrick. I don't need to remind you how grievously ill these men were." She scanned the room while soldiers dropped their eyes to avoid her gaze. "This is a hospital. Men die despite our best efforts. Contrary to being responsible for the deaths of these men, Mr. Penfold gave them a great gift." She stopped and stepped back, yielding the stage.

"Brave men," Penfold began. "I am saddened that you would think I meant harm to any one of you. But I understand that what occurred is hard to believe." He reached for the small mirror on his belt. It was an oval, about six inches tall and three inches wide, framed in wood with a wood cover that swiveled to cover the glass when not in use. He held it up, cover closed. "This mirror is an instrument of God!" His stentorian tone filled the room.

Murmuring began again, until Mrs. Forsythe motioned for quiet.

"This mirror was given to me by a dying soldier. He told me it allowed a glimpse of one's beloved. But only if that person were dying would the mirror work. You see, the mirror doesn't cause death but eases one's passing into the Heavenly Kingdom." Penfold raised his arms and eyes to the sky.

Rather than soothing the men, this revelation sent them into a panic. If Penfold approached them, they refused his visits and avoided eye contact just in case he offered the mirror. No dying man wants to believe he is dying. And the others weren't convinced that the mirror wasn't the cause of rather than the companion to the journey.

Instead of individual visits, Penfold began to lead daily morning prayers for all willing to attend. There was a surprisingly robust turnout. The soldiers wanted to keep a good relationship with God, as long as they weren't on the receiving end of individual attention from His messenger.

#

Hutchinson was firmly in the camp of those who suspected Penfold's mirror was assisting, if not directly causing, the deaths. An undercurrent of fear joined the feeling of unease he'd always had when in the vicinity of the tinker. Despite the fact that Penfold had never been anything but gracious to him, Hutchinson did not trust the man. He was more determined than ever to get out of the wheelchair and leave Abrams House, and Bartley Penfold, behind forever.

Hutchinson practiced using his crutch, at first by making his way around the ward several times a day. As he gained strength, he added a slow circuit of the grounds, which brought him past the tinker's forge tucked away near the barn. Mornings were ideal for his walks, since Penfold was busy leading prayers and Hutchinson never attended them anyway.

One gray morning after a heavy rain, Hutchinson crutched along the path with eyes downcast, careful to skirt large puddles but unable to avoid the thick mud. He sweated profusely in the cool air, working twice as hard to travel half as far, while the sucking mud yanked at his boot and attempted to wrest the crutch from his grasp. Stopping to catch his breath, he discovered he was right next to Penfold's wagon. The canvas sides were drawn down, as usual, but the back flap was rolled up.

Hutchinson's already rapid pulse increased at the opportunity to find out more about the tinker. He glanced around quickly, then moved closer and peered into the darkness inside. Shelves filled with jars and bundles lined the inside of the structure. His phantom right leg twitched with the desire to be of use, but the crutch was a poor substitute, and he could not climb the three steep steps to enter the wagon for a closer look.

"May I help you?" boomed a familiar voice behind him.

Hutchinson whirled. Or attempted to. The crutch skidded in the mud, and he lost his balance. His head cracked against the top step, and everything went black.

He awoke on a straw mattress, looking at a canvas ceiling. The smells of metal, Macassar oil, and damp assaulted his nostrils and he sneezed. An oil lantern provided dim light. Penfold's face filled his vision as the tinker leaned over him, brow furrowed with concern.

"Ah, there you are. You gave me quite a fright, Corporal."

Panicked at his vulnerable position, Hutchinson pushed up on his elbows, then fell back with a moan as his head exploded with pain.

"Doctor," he gasped.

"I've already sent for the doctor. He said not to move and that he would be here soon." Penfold stepped away. "Would you like something to eat? I'm afraid all I can offer is coffee and hardtack. I could have something brought from the house."

Hutchinson lay still, stomach churning and head pounding. "Not hungry," he said through clenched teeth.

Penfold returned to the bedside. He fondled the mirror hanging from his belt, running his fingers over the smooth wooden cover. Hutchinson quickly clamped his eyes shut. But rather than proffering the mirror, Penfold began to pray.

"Oh Lord, please heal this brave man, who has fought for you and for his country. Amen."

Too weak to resist years of habit, Hutchinson heard an automatic "Amen" come from his lips. He opened his eyes.

Penfold captured Hutchinson in his dark-eyed gaze. "While we wait for the doctor, I have a story to tell. Would you like to hear it?"

Trapped, Hutchinson willed his tongue to object, but it lay mute in his mouth like a somnolent slug. He tried to move his head only to find that paralyzed as well. What kind of magician was this strange man?

Penfold pulled the mirror from his belt and held it in front of Hutchinson's face, cover closed. With one slight movement of his thumb, he could expose the mirror and send Hutchinson to his death.

"God does not perform His miracles without cost," said the itinerant preacher. "Our faith He expects, but for some things He demands more. The cost for me has been to never stop moving, never have a home, to continually seek out souls to help. I must confess to feeling some envy for the men with families, who can view their loved ones for the final time. I have no one."

He stopped with a sigh, rubbed a hand over his smooth face then ran his fingers through jet-black hair. There had been two more deaths and Penfold now looked twenty years younger than when he had arrived. Even his yellow teeth had whitened.

When Penfold rubbed his face, he broke eye contact and thus released Hutchinson. The soldier rolled his head to the left to avoid being mesmerized again and spotted a row of glass jars on the shelves next to the bed. Penfold droned on, deep in his own world of self-pity. Hutchinson snaked his arm out from under the thin blanket and grabbed a jar, surprised at its weight. It rattled when he lifted it and Penfold turned toward him, but too late. Hutchinson smashed the jar against the side of the tinker's head. Penfold slumped across him with blood running from his temple.

Ignoring his own pounding head, Hutchinson pushed the man onto the floor and grabbed the camp mirror from his hand. He turned the surface away and slid the cover open. When Penfold groaned and awoke, he found himself staring directly into the magical mirror.

"No!" he screamed, scrabbling away until he bumped against the side of the wagon, unable to tear his eyes away. "I gave you a gift! All of you!"

Hutchinson continued to the hold the mirror in front of Penfold's face. The man's screams faded to whimpers, and he curled into a ball. Hutchinson watched in horror as Penfold's face returned to the wrinkled visage he'd had when he arrived at Abrams House. His black hair faded to iron gray and then went completely white. The man's hands bent into claws and his flesh seemingly melted away. With a final sigh, the skin-covered skeleton collapsed, to move no more.

Hutchinson shook his aching head, unable to believe what he'd just witnessed. Penfold's remains still sat slumped against the side of the wagon. Then he noticed white beads scattered around the body.

Were they what had rattled when he'd lifted the jar? He picked one up, examined it, then dropped it with a cry. A human tooth! He picked up another, and another. All teeth. He turned to the shelves and lifted a second jar close to his face. This one contained small bones—finger bones perhaps? A third jar held swatches of hair in all colors.

The man was a monster! The gruesome souvenirs exceeded even Hutchinson's worst nightmares. He lifted his crutch and brought it down on the cursed mirror, over and over until the glass was reduced to shards and the wood case to splinters. He pushed himself up on the crutch and moved the oil lantern to the top of the steps. After sliding down the steps on his belly, he threw the lantern back into the wagon, where the spilled oil quickly ignited.

He hurried away from the wagon as fast as his sore head and the still muddy ground would allow. When he arrived back at Abrams House, he told of Mr. Penfold accidentally dropping the lamp, then pushing him from the wagon before turning back to fight the fire. He'd barely escaped with his life. A column of black smoke rising above the trees lent truth to his tale. Mrs. Forsythe, with tears in her eyes, declared Penfold a godly man till the end, more concerned for others than himself. Hutchinson doubted the former owners of the teeth and bones would agree, but making Penfold out to be a hero drew attention (and suspicion) away from him.

The doctor, who had not in fact been summoned by Penfold, treated Hutchinson's injured head and prescribed a week of bed rest. During that week, Hutchinson had much time to think—many questions and few answers. Had the souls of the men Penfold ushered to their deaths appeared in the mirror when the tinker was forced to look into it? He couldn't be sure. Would Penfold have died from the blow or had Hutchinson killed him with the mirror? In either case, Hutchinson was responsible for the man's death. But he felt no guilt, just relief. And what did the jars of hideous trophies have to do with the mirror's magic, if anything?

Mrs. Forsythe held a grand funeral for the man, fortunately for Hutchinson while he was still on bed rest. She was more taken with Penfold than ever after his "heroic" death. At the week's end, Hutchinson insisted on leaving Abrams House. The place had been fouled by Penfold and he wanted nothing more to do with it. Mrs. Forsythe kindly gave him a small cart and pony for his travels, and he bade farewell to his temporary home.

#

Hutchinson traveled six miles the first day and set up camp in a sheltered grove. He built a fire and settled his bedroll next to it, feeling lucky to be alive. It would take another week or more to reach his family in the western part of the state. Only his mother and sister remained, and they had no idea he was coming home. He fell asleep smiling at the thought of surprising them.

He was awakened the next morning by something digging into his left hip. Reaching into his pocket, he pulled out a familiar-looking camp mirror. He screamed and threw it into the bushes. The next night, it returned to his pocket. He placed it in front of the cartwheels and ran over it. The next morning it was back. He left it at an inn, threw it in the fire, and tied it to a tree branch. It always came back.

He couldn't carry this cursed object to his family. His sister Margaret was a curious child. What if she found it and opened the cover? Maybe this was delayed justice for his murder of Penfold. In despair, he moved the cart off the path and tied the pony to a tree, sure that someone would find it and rescue the innocent animal. He gathered his few possessions and walked deep into the woods, where he built a fire and prayed for forgiveness.

After his final amen, he reached for the mirror and slid open the cover, hoping that his death would balance the scales of justice and end the curse. He looked into the glass, expecting the final comfort of a glimpse of his mother and sister. Instead, the mirror went black and Penfold's voice filled his head.

The next morning, a newly energized Hutchinson broke camp and walked out of the woods, using the crutch as skillfully as if he'd been born with it. He pulled himself onto the driver's bench of the cart and urged the pony north, toward battlefields filled with dying men.

Valerie B. Williams

Valerie B. Williams came late to writing but is making up for lost time. She has honed her craft through HWA's mentorship program (mentored by Tim Waggoner[1] in 2017), attending the Borderlands Press Writers Bootcamp[2] (2018 and 2019), and attending the Fright Club[3] online horror writers workshop (2018 and 2021). She continues to write and submit new stories, as well as completing and seeking publication for a supernatural thriller novel.

Several of Valerie's short horror stories have appeared in anthologies, including "Amazing Patsy" in *American Gothic Short Stories* (Flame Tree Press, 2019). Her most recent publication was the short story, "Oyster Hunt," in the January 2022 edition of Dark

---

1. https://timwaggoner.com/

2. https://www.borderlandspress.com/writers-boot-camp/

3. https://www.moanaria.com/frightclub

Recesses Press magazine. She lives near Charlottesville, Virginia, with her very patient husband and two equally patient Golden Retrievers.

Thank You for Reading

Refracted Reflections

If you liked it, please leave a review for the complete anthology or for any of the individual stories. Show your support for the wonderful authors whose stories are featured here.

Reviews are hugs for authors. Hug your authors!

HUGS

It's okay to post a review that's only about the stories that you read.

You may also like these other anthologies from *WordCrafter Press*

Once Upon an Ever After:
Twisted Myths & Shattered Fairy Tales
Purchase Link: https://books2read.com/u/mKdWGV

Whispers of the Past: https://books2read.com/u/38EGEL
Spirits of the West: https://books2read.com/u/ml2Kxq
Where Spirits Linger: https://books2read.com/u/mYGyNG

About the Publisher

About the Publisher

WordCrafter Press publishes quality books and anthologies. Learn more about *WordCrafter* and keep updated on current online book events, writing contests, up coming book blog tours and new releases on the *Writing to be Read* authors' blog: https://writingtoberead.com/

Lightning Source UK Ltd.
Milton Keynes UK
UKHW030633200922
409139UK00001B/70